Vindicare Hope
a Knights 15 13 short story
by Carl Michael Curtis

A Prequel

Cape and Swordstick Press

Gladstone, MO 64118

www.capeandswordstickpress.com

The characters and events in this book are fictitious. Any similarity to real persons, living or dead, is coincidental and not intended by the authors.

This is a work of fiction intended to be in communion with the Holy Catholic Church. It does not bear an imprimatur or a nihil obstat, but the authors have taken pains to ensure it does not conflict with anything the Church dogmatically teaches. If the authors have missed a detail that does conflict, the mistake belongs to the authors; The Holy Catholic Church does not teach error when it comes to faith and morals.

Cover art by Patrick Sayles

Cover and back cover layout and lettering by Paula Hays @ Floraliescreative.com

Copy editing by Catherine Lueckenette

Vindicare Hope
a Knights 15 13 short story
by Carl Michael Curtis

From Joe – to my mom, for always believing in me when I didn't believe in myself. And also to Ryan, for making this journey possible.

From Ryan – this one is for Donna, because she gets everything I do. And also, Doug F. and Luis B., two good partners who were sitting next to me as this story came together.

For he is God's minister to you for good. But if you do that which is evil, fear; for he bears not the sword in vain. For he is God's minister: an avenger to execute wrath upon him that does evil.

-Romans 13:4

Site of operations:

Klyfe Protos, fourth planet in orbit of G-Class star Vivae, Vivae-Kwov solar system

On-site resources:

Spec Ops Unit #3-3a, Lwanga, P. Commander

Saint Laurence, Eidolon-class stealth cruiser, Gibbons, M. Captain

3rd Commandry of the Knights of Those Washed in the Water and Blood from His Side ("Knights 15 13")

Mission details: stealth recovery and extraction of holy relics and other assets from enemy possession by any **just** means necessary in accordance with Knights 15 13 Rule of the Order, on body of dilatant fluid known locally as Devil's Throat Sea

Mission designation:

SANCTIONED by the Federal Interstellar Governmental Network/FedNET

SANCTIONED/UNSANCTIONED not applicable by planetary or local governments—threat operates in international waters, officially declared NOT OPPOSED TO actions by nearest national government, identified as nation of Thov

SANCTIONED/UNSANCTIONED not applicable by local solar system governmental authorities; none exist

SANCTIONED by Knights 15 13 Supreme Commandry in accordance with Decalogue commandments THOU SHALL NOT MURDER, THOU SHALL NOT STEAL, THOU SHALL NOT COVET THY NEIGHBOR'S POSSESSIONS

COMBAT PERMISSIONS:

Granted in full

Patron Saint(s) assigned to ops to request intercession from:

Saint Michael the Archangel (A*ngel,* eternal)

Saint Albinetine the hermit (*Homo Sapien, Ganymede, 2557-2621*)

Saint Charles the Thovic (*Homo Ursosus Thovicus, Klyfe Protos, 2695-2738*)

Miracles and Centuries Past

"The miracles given to all who will see, given through the power of the risen Christ Himself, those miracles are indisputable! So, see them, indeed! How can you doubt now?" The condemned man, known as Charles, shouted as he stood up from where the crowd shoved him down. Blood about his knees from where the executioner struck.

That executioner now, astonished and in disbelief, backed away. As did the whole crowd.

They had drug him to the main road, back in those days still made of cobble stones from the local Uro River. Just wide enough for their beasts of burden. Grasses would grow between the rocks and children would pick them, calling them trampling grasses and chewing on them as if they were sweetened by the feet of travelers.

Up and down the main road on both sides were small shops made from vanto wood and slab rock. In the middle of the day as it was then, there was bustling commerce, interrupted by the seething crowd who drug Charles to the square for execution.

This town, though near enough to a fledging monastery of Catholic monks, was feverishly resistant to their ideas of a godman named Jesus from another planet in another solar system in another time. The monastery had set up shop in enemy territory. Had been enduring persecution. And from a town far off down the road, an itinerant preacher named Charles had come to help lead the charge.

The sky was gray and gnarled—painted for murder. The crowd of Charles's species known as Thovics seized him. Brought him here to the main road. Forced him to his knees. Swung their decapitating knife at his throat. Now, silenced their cries for blood at him. Their thirst for it all was quenched, and their extreme fear began as Charles preached.

"I have come to preach of a loving God who asks you to step away from your deformed actions and give your life to Him! He desires us all to forever be in Communion with Him!"

A man in the crowd, butcher's knife in hand, his face quivered. Stunned by the sight before him, shock and disbelief in reality itself pushed him. He pointed knife at Charles and shouted, "Ghastly preacher! What evil animates you?"

"Not evil, but the Spirit of our Lord."

The executioner stammered. Could he really be having an argument with Charles? Even *now*? "You come to our town and preach against our gods! You blaspheme! The gods we have passed down for generations, the gods who saw us through famines and wars and—"

Charles waved away the question. "Those gods are not real and never have been. Why do you worship a bolt of lightning? Because it amazes you? Does it hear you? Does it speak your name to you in your prayers? Or a raging storm come down from the mountains that surges the tides up over our breakwaters? It has no power except that which is imbued in it by the One True God. Such power in those storms must belong to something greater than you, no? But these are not gods. The One True God I preach—"

"Our gods—"

"Are false!"

The crowd flinched at Charles. For weeks now he had been at the temple, arguing for the God of Christianity from the positions of reason and science. Logic. Saint Aquinas's five proofs of God's existence. The argument from contingency. Preaching from the sacred texts passed to them across the stars by Catholic missionaries.

Crowds argued him back, but fewer and fewer did so each week. They were refuted. More came to find him for personal conversations. Answers to whatever question stood in their way of accepting his beliefs. To confirm what they were being convinced of, that this One True God of his is real. That this Jesus he preached is real.

"Look at those who have converted!" Charles shouted. The crowd's fury had abated after he stood up. Whispers of Charles's next miracle was on their lips. Through his God he did incredible things. He had already healed several gravely ill people. Laid his hands on a lame child who threw down his walking stick and began running for the first time in his life. And now...

The Thovic with the butcher's knife lowered it. He had no more wind to power his fury. No one did. This blaspheming preacher had won.

Someone in the crowd swallowed hard and bluntly said, "His One True God is real."

Charles continued, "There are already churches in other towns, worshiping the One True God. You have a monastery not far from here, why do you not send your sons to it? Teach them to grow in holiness? Many of them could return to you and lead the generations towards God."

"How is this possible?" A woman in the crowd shrieked. She pointed at Charles, condemned to death by the governor. Drug to the execution site by this mob she was a part of. The self-appointed killer with the butcher's knife, bloody and dulled, in awe.

"The one true God conquered death!" Charles exclaimed, loud enough for his voice to carry into the hills. "For so many, He conquered it. Now, look. See for yourself."

Freshly decapitated, Charles turned a circle in the crowd. He used the hand not carrying his severed head to brush dirt from his knees. Straightened his garment. He stepped down off the execution mound and turned towards the monastery.

"We, who are trapped in our inequities, our lusts and hatred, our self-made filths, deserve nothing more than to be butchered here in this square as you have chosen to do to me. I am not clean, and I know this. The stain of sin soaks me to the bone. I choose it all the day, and how I despise my weakness for it. Though, I know I am loved. Loved by God. What can I do but try and master myself to allow Him to work through me? Sin has worked through me; how much greater it is that God does too! He loves me and you alike! You can be saints, as I am striving to be!

Why can none of you see that? Why will none of you allow yourselves to be comforted by that? Feast your eyes and know the truth I speak! Repent! I love you all, and wish to be in paradise with you."

The crowd parted, allowing the decapitated preacher to amble forward along the road. His head, cradled in one arm, preached and preached the love and forgiveness of the One True God. He stopped, stooped and plucked a blade of trampling grass from between the stones. Kept walking towards the monastery on the horizon and the Thovic around him stayed ever quieter in their shock. One man fell to his knees, the miracle of God before him too much to ignore. He began crying, pleading for forgiveness for the murder in his heart. Then a woman fell to her knees, and another man. Then they fell by twos and threes.

Charles the Thovic continued shouting a single mantra like a responsorial psalm in the Mass, "Praise to our lord, Jesus Christ, King of Endless Glory! He, fully human and fully divine, with power over death itself! Let me praise His name forever and ever, amen!" on down the road until he disappeared from their sight.

Brilliant Blue and Discomforted Hearts

Flames follow him closely as he traces the trails of blood on the ancient stone floor.

The Saint Albertine Monastery has stood for millennia, even before the men of this God took it over two centuries prior. Before the Christians came, it was a Thovic equivalent of a castle, when their continent was the breeding grounds of an ancestor of the giant plains lizards. Though hunted to extinction here, they are still in existence across the sea. In the lands of the Hhrothgar people.

But now, instead of guarding against those massive four-legged serpents or the marauders of days past, the monastery stands as a monument to the Creator of the universe, and both His love and glory.

It *was* a monument. Now, it is little more than bloody rubble and a burning pit. It is a robbed grave.

The Hhrothgar raiders that sailed in under cover of predawn darkness, now in morning's light they move about the collapsed rafters, the smashed walls, going chamber to chamber. Executing any survivors. Pillaging. But alone, this crew member, new to the pirates, keeps his gun holstered. His blade sheathed.

He passes through the open courtyard and past the overturned statue of an alien woman clutching flowers to her breast. Draped in a blue and white robe, cracks like fault lines running through her. "A new low for disrespect," he says. He picks up an errant chunk of the statue and walks over to it. Like a puzzle piece, he sets it back in the crevice where it broke off. Goes inside.

From room to room, he turns over the freshly dead Thovic monks. Examines them the way one does an important photograph, scrutinizing for details. Intently. He kneels to one monk slain in a hallway and takes hold of his jaw. Turns his face this way and that. As he does, two of his ship's crew come around the corner. One wipes blood off his blade, the other eating a piece of food stolen from the dead Thovic somewhere behind.

"Oy, First Mate. Why you runnin' him one over?" The one cleaning blood asks. "Ain't he dead already?"

The Hhrothgar first mate shrugs. Lies. "You never know."

The one cleaning his blade makes one final wipe and sheaths it. Comes over to the first mate and draws a pistol. Shoots the dead monk through the forehead. "There. Now we knows, eh?" He begins laughing. The other laughs and spits his half-chewed food out. The first mate gives a chummy but limp snicker and urges them away.

When they continue their cackling and round the next corner, the first mate says, "Fools."

He comes into a larger room with several corpses. Overturned tables and spilled food. Crusts half chewed. Jeffa buds, those small yellow fruits from a local orchard pebbled along the floor like a handful of thrown sand. The spilled bowl they cascaded out from smashed like the dreams these monks had. A pitcher of water cracked and leaking, mixing with blood.

The first mate moves one body, cloaked in a simple tunic with a corded belt and examines his face. Moves to the next. After the third he turns and sees a Thovic brother sitting up against a broken table. Hand over a chest wound, staunching his life from slowly leaving him. Looking right at the Hhrothgar raider. "Checking their heritages?" he asks in a breathless voice. No fear in his eyes.

"That I am," the first mate says. The room is large—dining hall, by the obviousness of it—but they are the only two left living. The first mate cannot stop the injured monk from dying. His wound, center of his chest, the way the blood is rushing around his fingers, it is no use. Maybe if this was a hospital he'd have a chance, but doubtful. There is an easiness between them, because there is no pretense.

"What for? Distant family, I presume."

"One my mother's side," The Hhrothgar says. The Thovic and Hhrothgar are cousins, split by the Devil's Throat Sea. Once a common people, as the tribes migrated to the east and west, around the sea and into their separate worlds, they branched into their distinctive modern-day forms.

"Do you know his name?" the monk asks. "The brother you seek?"

"No," the first mate says. "But his a'tai is like mine." He motions to the space above his nose and between his eyes. Its pattern of wrinkle and swirl, plus the small horns sprouting there, nothing more than a few millimeters, they read like fingerprints to the peoples of both sides. Unmistakable.

"Come closer," the dying monk says. He beckons him with a single inviting wave of his free hand.

The Hhrothgar pauses to scan for a trap. Maybe this monk is bloodthirsty, wanting to take even a single enemy with him to the grave.

The monk notices, and smiles. "Fear not, friend. I mean you no harm."

"Hard to believe with the current state of things."

"But you must believe it. It hurts to speak. Come, come. Before I go."

The first mate approaches, leans in and lets the monk see. The monk squints to study it, then nods with recognition. Looks around from corner to corner. His brothers in every conceivable position but upright. Points with a drooping arm to the far corner. "Bav. The Lord wills you to find him. Bav was dining with us when your men arrived. Instead of. . . anywhere else, I suppose. Over there."

The Hhrothgar follows the monk's finger, absently says, "Bav," speaking his distant relative's name for the first time, for the last time.

"Tell me why, though," the monk says. "We are all related. If not by blood such as you and he, by our Eternal Father, through whom all are made possible."

The Hhrothgar considers the question, hearing a gunshot in the background. Down the hall. "I am new to these people, this crew. You know the Hhrothgar. We are a culture far apart from you Thovic. We must do what we must do, but I am— my heart does not like it."

"Why do you seek him? Bav?"

"Shared blood, I suppose. To apologize, perhaps. I am called to it from a voice only I can hear." The first mate stands and goes over to Bav's body. His dead relative lays sprawled on the floor, a spoon still in his hand. The first mate can see his a'tai, see his family in it. He kneels over him and runs a hand down his face, moving his eyelids closed. "To your god, I commend you," he says, and gazes upon him for a moment. He sees a string of beads cascading out of Bav's garment. Out of a pocket hidden inside the folds of it.

He pulls the beads out and finds a ring of them. Attractive. A single string dangles off, and at the end of it a decoration. Two lines crossed over one another, with a male of another species attached to it. He has seen it on the walls in this monastery, an icon of their god, he presumes.

He has heard stories of how Thovics from long ago would not accept these images. Too foreign; a male of another species was something they could not connect to. Some apologists for the religion argued that since this was His image, it should stay. Others suggested to add Thovic details to His image in order to make it familiar.

Just walking through here, Agravain has seen both, and in his hands, evidence that Bav accepted his God as He was.

The cord itself is black. The beads are a brilliant glossy blue. It has a few other adornments; a metal oval with the bust of some person on it—this one a Thovic holding his head in his hands. Knots tied along it between numerous series of beads. The first mate stands with it in his hand and the dying monk says, "Ah, Bav's rosary."

The first mate walks back over, asks, "What is it?"

"A gift for you. We use it to pray."

"It is nonsense."

The monk smiles and winces. "Look around you. Peaceful, good men. They all dedicated their lives to the human you see on that cross. They died for their love for Him. That might be nonsense, but I do not think so. Bav did not think so. And whatever voice drew you here to find him, to commend him to his God, that does not think so. Listen to it. It loves you."

The first mate stares, curling the rosary up in his palm.

"Agravain, what are you doing?" The captain's voice demands from behind.

The first mate turns, startled. "Skipper, I. . . am looking for anything of value to the markets back home."

"Is this a dining hall?" The captain stands in the doorway, Thovic blood smeared over him. In his hand his ceremonial sword, known as a grunta. He gazes at Agravain with what feels like so much hatred.

"Aye, skipper. It appears so, yes."

"Are their bread crusts going to fetch my crew a handsome reward? These squashed jeffa?"

"No."

"Then stop wasting time. I have gotten what I wanted. Tell the crew we push off at dusk. Stragglers get left behind."

"Aye, skipper."

The captain begins to leave but turns around, smirks. "Oh. And, we have another stop to make. I marked it on the charts. More cargo. Set course for it. I want to be there tonight." The captain turns and leaves. Agravain waits until he is gone and returns his attention to the dying monk.

"Be a straggler, my brother." the monk says, so weak are that the words and composed of gentle coughs and whispers. "No good comes from. . . following evil."

"It is my job now."

"Following the One True God is your job. Nothing else, ever."

Agravain scoffs. "I have seen no such thing."

"You will, brother. As Bav did before you."

Agravain lets the prophecy spend too much time in his thoughts, and he cannot stop the words as they come out. "If I did see this One True God, I'd like to think I'd recognize Him."

No response. Agravain looks to the monk. Sees him lying still, a smile on his face. His limp hands slid down his front until they rest at his side. Agravain nudges him with a foot. He does nothing.

Agravain wonders why he said such a thing about a god he does not believe in. Looks around to see if the words were magically floating in the air for someone else to see and reveal his inner thoughts. They would kill him, for sure. But he is alone.

"Never mind." Rosary in hand, discomfort in his heart, Agravain leaves the dining hall. Somewhere else far away inside the monastery, he hears another gunshot.

Holy Blood and Preaching Skulls

The Hhrothgar captain stands on the bow of his ship, the dry wind coming off the Devil's Throat Sea blowing through the quills on his head and beard, rattling the ceremonial war beads he is adorned with. His prideful snarl brighter than the sun.

The ship is forged using the skeleton of a giant plains lizard for frames and a keel. The skeleton, bones of onyx black, is transported from wherever among the tall grasses the lizard dies and laid out in their shipyard to be cleaned. Every scrap of flesh is removed. The belly outfitted with metal planks, machinery and a nuclear reactor situated on desk inside the massive swell of hip, driving its leg bones in a cycling action to propel the corpse-turned-vessel through the thick muck of sea.

The captain is fascinated by the sound that same dry wind makes as it travels through the eye sockets of the skull in his hands. A raiding prize. Supernatural.

Noises like a song, maybe. Or a voice preaching. Speaking to him.

The skull is Thovic, old and the dull gray of iron ore. The captain holds the bone up into the open air and faces it forward, giving the winds unfettered access. How they swirl into the sockets, the nasal cavity, whirl around inside the brain case. A beautiful, haunting sound like blowing into a conch shell.

The Devil's Throat Sea expands out all around him and his crew and his ship. Nearly three hundred kilometers across and one hundred wide, the sea separates two of the largest continents on the planet Klyfe Protos. Instead of a life-giving water, however, it is a body of non-Newtonian fluid completely captured by the continents; it lays flat except how the wind coming off the northern mountains blow ropy film off the top of its surface. Those mountains, a blurry mark along the horizon, a world off.

There is no tide. No waves. The worst are those ropy films which are shoveled up in great drifts by the winds and rolled for a moment or two before they get too heavy. Too implacable. And they melt back into the lifeless sea. Even the great sea cutters that carve their way across the Devil's Throat Sea throw a wake that is merely a single ripple and then flattened.

Every vessel on the sea must be extremely buoyant. Must constantly power through the bizarre, quicksand-like moat. For a vessel to stop its forward momentum is to risk sinking. There is no aquatic life swimming under its currents. Nothing can breathe the starch-like suspension.

The sky above is a deep jewel blue, littered with thin streaks of iridescent clouds. High noon is coming upon them, and the captain takes a bead off his war decoration and hurls it sidelong across the sea. It hits hard, skips off the surface in more of a thud than anything precise or graceful. Skips two more times before settling into the sand-colored fluid and stops cold. As the non-Newtonian fluid loses viscosity around it, it flows more like a true liquid and the bead sinks. Gone.

"Why did they treasure it so, skipper?" Agravain, asks as he approaches from the aft. He looks at the skull and darts his eyes away. Something about it has made all the crew do that. A prize that most of them don't want on the ship with them. But to Agravain, something else. Something he is not ready to face just yet.

"I presume they think it is magic or some sort of nonsense," Captain Melligrance says in his deep, slithering voice. His mane of quills shivers as he regards the bones. "I hope it fetches an impressive price when I sell it. Maybe a ransom, instead? Their abbot protected it to his death, and such a pity. I had hoped to sell him as well."

He turns the skull in his hand, the smear of dried blood from the abbot's death wound still tacky on it. Captain Melligrance looks at the skull face on, and his eyes dart away from making contact with the empty sockets.

"We are a superstitious lot, skipper."

"You're a lot of whatever I tell you to be."

"Aye, skipper. We are that too."

On his ship, in the open air, under the golden sunlight. He withdraws a flask and drinks from it. Rests a hand on his gun, then moves it to his sword. Both slung around his waist, both won from Hhrothgar warriors he brutally defeated in combat. The sword is old enough to have been taken from multiple warriors, passed down by bloody hand to bloody hand as its previous owner fell to the wrath of its next. It is their way.

"When will be in port, Agravain?"

The first mate, whose quills are shorter than the captain's by half and lusterless white, without the ringing colors that the more aggressive Hhrothgar males have, looks to the northwest. Squints. "Before nightfall, captain. Middle dusk."

The captain, whose quills are ringed by thick bands of brilliant crimson reds, bone whites, azure blues and thin black, looks the same direction. Squints as well. "No, we won't."

Agravain fights the look of humiliation from his face. Tries to keep his stoicism from melting. "I see the Hurrum Point, captain, right there." He gestures to a slab of rock forty meters high coming out of the sea but he will not meet the captain's eye. "From it, only another bit to the port. Maybe two dhars. Maybe. Before nightfall, though."

"That is Skurrum Point, the sister rock to Hurrum Point. Its base is fatter, its tip curled like a hook. Half a dhar between them, and then three dhars to the port. Go inspect the charts again and earn your position under my flag."

In Agravain's ears, almost inside his mind, he hears the wind pass through the skull. A whisper. *Return to the God of your forefathers.* He focuses on that for a moment, and—

"I will not repeat myself," Captain Melligrance growls. The fury in his eyes is enough to stoke the reactor behind them.

"Aye, skipper," Agravain says, clearing his mind. He turns around. His quills deflate, lay flat along his head, neck and back.

"First mates aren't hard to come by, Agravain," the captain says with a looming threat in his voice like deep black storm clouds on the horizon. "Neither are slaves in my holds. When Captain Forgah recommended you to me, I wondered then as I do now if he just wanted you off his crew and he knew I'd wind up killing you. Keep that in mind, eh?"

"Aye, skipper," he says again, all the strength drained from it, and Agravain hurries off before he hears more horrible things. Captain Forgah ran a commercial ship hauling minerals and nectars, not this kind of raiding vessel. Being a first mate there was no different, but this kind of bloodtrade gives the ship a haunted, cursed aura. Horrible things, indeed.

Captain Melligrance turns back to the bow. The wind still blowing through the skull. He looks at it, hears that supernatural sound in the music of it all. A voice. Holds it up to his ear. The sound stops, as if it will only speak to him if they are eye to eye. He turns the skull towards his mouth like a hungry man holding an apple, and he licks the tacky blood off it in one long, lusty motion.

"I've always enjoyed holy blood," he says to the skull. His quill beard jingling with its husky rattle. "Almost like your fake god is in the droplets, and it tastes like my own glory, since I have spilled that blood."

Inside the skull he can see a shape etched into it. A long horizontal line with a shorter diagonal one crossing it. The same thing the abbot had on himself as he perished. As he bled that holy blood.

Captain Melligrance withdraws his grunta and sets the skull on the end of it. Holds it up in the air and lets the wind make its noise in the cavities.

Two Clones and Many More Relics

Inside a submersible, special operations detachment #3-3a of Those Washed in the Water and Blood from His Side do the last of their checks as they set course for the Hhrothgar ship. They were inserted on the north side of Skurrum Point the night before and made their way to the southern side of it in the morning. Aerial reconnaissance pinpointed the enemy vessel the previous day and determined its speed and heading, and now the submersible is heading on the very same track line, opposite course.

"Okay. Showtime is upon us," Commander Lwanga says as checks the safety on his rifle. Pacing back and forth in the two square meters he has at the front of the conference room, he addresses his Knights. "This ship and crew raided Saint Albinetine's monastery on the northern coast of Thov yesterday morning. Father Josephus called them something like Vikings. From Earth. I don't know. I've never been."

Brothers Becket, Thomas, Clotilde, Scammacca, Magallenes and Bosco geared up in their stealth armor, all having to lean over slightly due to the tightly enclosed space of the submersible. This compartment is what serves as a conference room, and it is slight enough to where they cannot sit down. Nor is there a table to sit at. There is little more than seven men in a can.

"It was in the brief, but the background again for the sake of being thorough: the nation of Thov is the most solidly Catholic one on this planet and has been for a little over the last three centuries. Evangelists didn't make many inroads on the other continents but after Saint Charles's evangelization, they were well received in Thov. And that was good; Thov boasts almost a full third of the planet's sentient population and they're peaceful. Side note—the continent is called Ursosus, but Thov takes up most of its landmass. Saint Albinetine's monastery has been a fixture on the coastal hillside for something like three hundred years. Very holy place. Now it's mostly ashes and dried blood.

"These bad guys, they're Hhrothgar, which is a pagan warrior culture from the western hemisphere. Side note—when the evangelists traveled there all those years ago, they were expecting a harder sell than they had on Thov, and we must assume they faired rather poorly." Lwanga eyeballs his Knights dourly. "They disappeared. No one ever heard from the again."

"I thought all New World Evangelists had embedded transponders?" Clotilde asks.

"They do, yeah. Went dark," Lwanga says and shrugs. "But immediately murdering strangers sounds like it's in line with the Hhrothgar way of life. What the brief says."

"Ah. Great."

Lwanga clears his throat. "Anyway, Same general species as those from the eastern hemisphere, Thov and the monks at Saint Albertine's. Hhrothgar are ruthless, their entire culture is built around strength and aggression. I've never run into them personally, but the mission brief is very clear. There are no negotiations. Thovic authorities have already tried to make contact. Make an arrangement of some kind. The Hhrothgar don't deal. At best, they might try to ransom some items back to the Thovic. Might. If we're discovered, only death will end the engagement. Ours or theirs."

The Knights nod, well aware of the risks. Lwanga has his way of doing things, and his Knights are well aware of that too. They've read the read the mission details in their Visuals, but Lwanga will present it along with his plan, requirements, expectations, all of it. Generally, he presents it as if they did not receive it and instead, woke up a few hours before the operation just to find themselves somehow involved.

"So, pretty simple," he continues. "They're towing a large crate of the loot they took, including relics. We breach the surface behind the crate, enter it, confirm the contents and then begin sneaking them off onto the submersible. Once it's empty, we dive. Go to the exfil site."

Lwanga examines a message thread they've received as new intel comes in. "I guess they hit the monastery, then moored alongside another vessel afterwards. Intel seems to think they took on additional cargo since then. We'll have to be flexible when we surface."

"Why not just air strike the ship and haul off the crates, sir?" Becket asks.

"One, we don't know their capabilities," Lwanga says as he holds up his thumb. "Like I said, they've already met up with another vessel like them. Intel thinks they're still in the general area and will probably respond to a distress call." He adds his pointer finger, "Two, the Hhrothgar culture will see that as a brazen act of war. If they don't know to blame the Order, intel says they'll most definitely blame the Thovic for it, since it was they who were raided."

"All-out war. I see."

Lwanga holds up his middle finger as well, "Three, I know they're aggressive and murderous, but there's some clerical dispute whether or not we could just surprise attack and kill them as they sit, unawares. At least, in this situation. Just War Theory and all."

"I think it's clear enough, but—"

"But you're not a cleric in our chain of command."

Becket shrugs. "No, sir."

"Will we plant explosives on the ship, sir?" Thomas asks.

"Same answer as to Becket," Lwanga says. "Thov has, of course, asked us to go ahead and wipe the ship off the map. So far, command has said they can fight their own war if it means that much to them. Culturally, the Hhrothgar and Thovic have these little incursions—mostly instigated by the Hhrogar, and they go back millennia. We're not keen on jumping in if it's not absolutely necessary.

"No word if we might be able to justify it morally because they are particularly unrepentant and vicious pirates—their livelihood is raping, pillaging and murdering—but the primary goal is the relics recovery. They took art, statuary, the whole bit."

"Might be better to just detonate the ship and tow the crate back ourselves," Becket says. "If that's—"

"We're not murderers, and this is not a democracy." Lwanga says. "We're done with that conversation."

"I'm not saying we should be—"

"This goes according to plan," Lwanga says and moves on as if Becket wasn't left hanging. "Recover the relics onto our submersible."

Becket leans over to Clotilde. "We got enough room for all that here?"

Clotilde smirks and shrugs. "Might have to pick and choose, man. I don't know."

Lwanga overhears them. "Brother Becket, another question for the operation?"

Becket shapes up. "No, sir. I was just wondering if we'll be able to fit all that into the submersible."

"So, you do have a question."

"Well, yes sir, I guess I do, if it's like—"

"The submersible was selected with the stolen items in mind. Did you read the brief?"

"Yes, sir."

While the entire team is watching Becket answer, Thomas feels guilty. Before he can think better of it, he blurts out, "Commander Lwanga, maybe I was taking up all of Becket's time earlier when we should have been reading—" Lwanga turns to Thomas, raises an eyebrow.

"Did you read the brief *for* Becket?"

"No, sir. Well— I mean, yes sir. Most of it, sir. But not *for* Becket, sir. He read it, too. I just—"

"Did you distract Becket from reading it?"

Thomas glances to Becket, who's expression is more defiant than stoic. He does not glance back. "Sir, I... I'm not sure?"

Lwanga groans. "Brother Thomas, this is your first op as a Knight so I'll forgive you, just as our Lord does. But I will also instruct you as our Lord does. We're special forces, not ditch diggers. We don't just show up for the day's work. We plan ahead, we know our op inside and out, our objectives, our details, our everything. We know our reaction plans inside and out. Do I need to keep going? No? Good. We also do not distract one another from preparing. That will get us all killed."

"I know, sir, I just—"

"No," Lwanga says, holding up a hand to silence him. "No. You must *not* know, because if you *did* know, you wouldn't have done it. So, zip it and learn from it."

"Yes, sir."

Lwanga turns back to Becket and purses his lips. "*You* do know better, Brother Becket. But since you're worried the Knights 15 13 did not allow for enough space to reacquire what a monastery full of monks were brutally murdered over, you can be the one to go topside and verify."

"Yes, sir."

"You still hold the seminary record for hand-to-hand combat, is that correct?"

Becket smirks. "Last time I checked, Commander. The Takayama style, yes."

"Good. Is stealth a part of that martial art? Because we need that. A lot. This mission should be accomplished without us even bringing weapons."

"No, sir. It's a mixture of offensive and defensive. It's technically there for when things like stealth and diplomacy fall short."

"Never mind, then." Lwanga takes in a deep breath through his nostrils and grits his teeth. "Okay, and one more thing—"

A chime rings through the submersible. Lwanga turns his head to a display on the bulkhead near him. A message reads out. He stares at it, holds up a single finger to his men indicating for them to wait, then tilts that finger until he's pointing at them. Steps nearer the message.

The submersible has a small buoy dragged by a cable on the surface of the Devil's Throat Sea. The buoy is designed like a long, thin knife to create a minimal wake, and in the non-Newtonian fluid any wake is extremely minimal to begin with. The buoy serves as a message relay between the Knights and their aerial support.

Lwanga reads the message and drops his head. Turns around. "All right. That was the *Saint Laurence.* Some kind of communications card or a box or something critical on board just faulted and fried out. They thought they had a spare but it turns out that one was the spare. They went into orbit so they could float. I guess that comms card is crucial to their drive or nav or something. Their guys can fix it but we don't have support until they do, and that'll be in about twelve hours."

Scammacca halfway raises a hand, asks, "Scrapping the mission, sir?"

"No."

"Roger."

Lwanga shakes his head, sets his face determined. "Nope. By the time the *Saint Laurence* gets back to mission ready, the Hhrothgar vessel will be safely in port and offloading." Lwanga wags his eyebrows. "We'll just have to be extra sneaky." He clears his throat and rolls his head on his shoulders. "All right. Final checks. Then be ready to deploy in five. That'll give us enough time to say some devotional prayers before we start."

Lwanga eyes his team and runs a hand across his scalp, then tents his fingers in front of him. "All right. Now listen up. I want this thing to go smooth and by the numbers. This is our chance to prove ourselves. A new team, and the last op didn't go well. Losing Brother John-Paul only two missions into our formation is a heavy burden. But we're back, and we're more than capable. So please, let the Lord guide you. Stay in prayer, keep your head in the game and do not deviate from the plan. Ask Brother John-Paul to pray from the feet of our Lord for intercession. We're going to nail this thing and then we'll have a solid victory behind us. Got it?"

The Knights nod. They know their commander doesn't want anything more.

"Good. Good," Lwanga twirls a finger in the air as he adopts a serious look. "Get on with it, then."

The Knights relax as Lwanga walks forward into the nose compartment. Becket turns and sees Thomas staring at him, a sorrowful pull to his face. Becket smiles, walks over. "Don't worry, Thomas. The commander is a good guy; he's just stern."

Thomas tries to return the smile. "I just feel bad. I wasn't trying to sell you out."

"You didn't. I read the mission brief, but Lwanga's biggest fault might be he only hears what he wants to hear... and believe me. That's *all* he hears."

"Lord, please forgive me for saying this, but I thought maybe he's got something against clones."

Becket nods. "A lot of people do have something against us, but I've never seen it in Commander Lwanga. I've never seen it in the Knights 1513. Guys like you and me, we wouldn't be here without the Knights."

"I know."

Becket taps an insignia he has on his armor of a petri dish inside a stylized outline of human uterus. "There's got to be thousands of versions of me out there right now. Created in a lab, sold as a slave, a laborer, a soldier, a servant, a test subject, whatever. And God loves all of us uniquely and fully. But you and me—" he taps the same insignia on Thomas, "—we get be Knights 15 13. We are blessed."

Thomas nods. "I think about it often. How I was rescued out of a science lab, waiting my turn to be grown enough for them to harvest my cells or organs or whatever they could plan."

"Yup." Becket says. "But here we are now. In a submersible that apparently has enough room for a monastery's worth of objects. With five other men who literally slept shoulder to shoulder last night with our knees up to our chins. With one portable toilet that will need to be shot into the sun by the op's end."

Thomas laughs and it feels good. It peels off some of the guilt he carries.

Becket nods solemnly. "And anyways, we're in good hands with our Lord. If you can't shoulder the burden by yourself, He will help you. I've learned that time and time again."

"Amen to that."

Becket turns to the rear compartment where the other Knights went. "All right, brother. Let's go recover some stolen relics and whatnot."

Dilatant Fluids and Empty Magboots

Inside the submersible Brother Becket waits at the bottom of the ladder well that leads to the topside hatch. He stands at the ready, praying the Athanasian Creed. A resounding metallic clank like the staccato death peel of some dying church bell rings through the vessel. He takes a deep breath.

Commander Lwanga's voice comes over the comms. "Magna-lock to the crate is effective. We're reeling in. Standby; we'll be shutting down our propulsion as soon as we're in final position."

Becket climbs to the top of the ladder, poised under the hatch. One hand on it. He can feel the subtle shift in the submersible's forward motion. They matched the Hrothgar's vessel speed; station-keeping under where the crate should be. Now locked on, they can conserve fuel.

Brother Thomas appears below. "Becket, you think us adding our weight to their tow will alert them that something's wrong?"

"Intel says the nuclear drive they have shoving them through this goop, that drive just puts out huge amounts of torque. I guess there's some spots that are more or less viscous than others, so it just automatically adjusts to resistance, and they keep going. Our drag should register to them as more viscous fluid, is all."

"I've been reading up on that goop. It's a non-Newtonian fluid. Specifically, a dilatant."

"Yeah, I didn't get that far."

"Well, non-Newtonian fluids are fluids that don't conform to Newton's law of viscosity, which is consistent viscosity independent of stress. Shearing rates—"

"Okay," Becket says. "I believe you studied up on it."

"It's just that, well, dilatants, their viscosity increases when stress acted upon it increases. You know, it'll flow like a fluid when left to its own devices but when you stress it, like punch it or run a paddle through it, it toughens up. A lot. There's your resistance and corresponding increase in torque."

"Like our sub," Becket nods. "Okay, well. Intel says the Hhrothgar will think dragging us is just a thicker spot in the dilatant. They won't bat an eye. Perfectly normal here. We're taking advantage."

"Okay." Thomas looks nervous. "The commander is going to let me be the next up after you."

"It'll be fun."

"You think so?"

Becket shrugs. "Yeah. Why not?"

"Becket?" The commander's voice again over their comms.

"Yes, sir?"

"Are you at the hatch?"

"Yes, sir."

"We'll surface in five seconds. Be prepared to exit in seven, only on my mark."

"Yes sir."

It's a seven-second count that simultaneously feels like one second and an eternity. Lwanga's firm single word, "Mark," a stab into the world of otherwise silence, comes across the comms and Becket yanks the dogging handle on the hatch. He eases it up, and with his active camo on, he emerges into the sunlight. Into the immediate shadow of a giant dull metallic box a meter before him.

The air rolls over in a steady way; too strong to be a breeze but not enough roar to be a good wind. It smells yeasty. Thick. Becket looks around and sees the vast sea, sand-colored and flat. A desert-like nothingness that would only move if beaten upon.

The nearly cloudless sky overhead. The sun like some great divine eye. The unnerving pulse of the nuclear drive somewhere ahead of him, hidden safely behind the crate. The Devil's Throat Sea begrudgingly sluicing around the hatch base. He climbs up and out, looks at the crate.

Along the top of it are large rectangular air vents. Evenly spaced from side to side, he shrugs. "Easier than cutting through it, if even just for a moment."

He maglocks to the side and climbs up to the nearest vent. A gentle clang with each contact, he pauses after the first two. Making sure they're not so loud as to tip off the Hhrothgar somehow. When he's convinced no lookout has heard him, he eases and climbs up the final several paces. Peers in. The stench hits him, even through his helmet.

Wall to wall, front to back, terrorized faces stare up at the air vents from a meter below. Dirty. Bloody. Demoralized. Male and female, child and adult. All with feverous eyes looking everywhere at the vents for whatever made that rhythmic clanking sound climbing up.

Whoever made it.

Hope, almost feral, spreads like wildfire. Fear also.

"Hello?" Someone asks from inside in a croaky, harsh voice. Becket's universal translator clicks on with static as the word is worked out. Becket doesn't know if these people are just parched and extremely weary and that's why they sound so gruff, or if it is a standard element to their species. He's betting dehydrated. Suffering. "Hello? Is someone there? Oh, please, please help us."

A rising murmur of begging begins. Crescendos. Thirty? Forty? A hundred voices join in, hushed whispers groaning and pleading so vigorously, so dejected that their collective muzzled cries become loud in unified effort.

Becket ducks down under the vent. Urgently, "Commander, you read me?"

"Yes, Becket."

"Sir, this crate is full of people."

"People?"

"Yes sir. Thovic captives. They're packed in there so tight they can't bend over."

"Send me a picture."

Becket leans up and uses his Visuals system to photograph the clutch of Thovic prisoners. He transmits it down into the submersible. Thovics, bipedal humanoids, characterized by extra-long, thin ears that run from the crowns of their heads to their jaw hinges. Their extremely high cheek bones, their almost absent chins. Large black eyes. Very similar to their species-cousins, the Hhrothgar, although the Hhrothgar have greenish mottled skin and their quills. The northern Thovic are deeply rusty in complexion and skin smooth as silk.

In a moment, Lwanga asks, "Is there another crate?" What's the layout?"

Becket tries very hard—though he knows it is completely in vain—to maglock climb around the crate without all the noise from before. He makes it to the edge, sees it. A second crate spaced off to the Hhrothgar ship's port side. He climbs up on top of the crate and sees a third crate over on the starboard side.

"Commander, there's two more. We're on the centerline one. The other two are spaced out on either side. No air vents on them, though. That's probably our monastery loot."

"Intel said so, yes. It was in the brief."

"Copy," Becket realizes he's speaking louder. Over the growing rumble inside the crate. "You guys gotta be quiet," he says to himself. He can't speak their language. He shushes, loud enough to hear a reaction inside. Like pressing silence down into the crowd and rolling it around. Quiet where it lay, but everywhere else there was bubbling murmuration.

"I'm coming up there." Lwanga says, and Becket looks down to the hatch.

†

Marhault knows better than to be a fool a second time.

To a Hhrothgar male, suffering a bad death was preferable to living a bad life. Reacting poorly to surprising events led to foolish decisions.

Being a fool led to humiliation. Humiliation led to a bad life. A bad life has led Marhault to where he's been for the past season.

When his quills, which were rich and vibrant before his foolishness, had been clipped off before the entire ship's crew as part of his discipline, Marhault wanted to die in combat rather than endure being reduced to the level he went to. He still grits his teeth at it, burns inside.

There was a slave uprising a season prior. They were newly captured, and still on the high water. A day out from port, they were still inside the old slave crates and the captives began running amok, so the Hhrothgar crew had to pacify the revolt without ruining the merchandise. Marhault underestimated a slave as he went to retake possession of him. The slave had set a booby trap with a line under tension, and as Marhault got close enough to lay hands on him, the slave cut the line. Sailors call it snapback. The line, so taut it could be a piano string, severed and snapped across the deck.

The slave chose certain death over a life of forced servitude and was cleaved in half by the line. Marhault lost his arm below the elbow.

That slave was the only one who died; the rest were pummeled into submission and tied for the remainder of the journey. As Captain Melligrance was ceremonially shaving Marhault's head of his quills, then shaving his beard of the same, he said, "That one slave was worth the price of your compensation for two entire seasons. One slave for two seasons. Maybe I don't pay you enough, but why would I pay more? You walked into an obvious trap and cost all of us—all your shipmates, your sailing vessel, *your captain*—an egregious amount. The embarrassment alone makes my stomach oily."

He held the quill knife to Marhault's throat, "Or maybe you'd make a better slave?"

"No."

"We will get better crates for our slaves," Melligrance announced, "And *you* will have stern watch for two entire seasons."

And Marhault is there now, on the stern. Staring aft, as he stands on a platform above the nuclear drive. The winds run along up and around his back and do not disturb his quills too much because they have only grown back in as stubble. The blaring hum of the reactor consuming the world. The clink and clank of the massive rotor gears that the drive turns, and those turn the dead skeletal legs whose feet slap the Devil's Throat Sea with immense power. That slap increases the viscosity of the dilatant fluid, allowing it to push off from the suddenly firm surface. The nose knifes through, the ballasts hold the belly afloat and the feet slap again.

Marhault sees the central crate where the slaves are. On the towing cable, thirty meters off the stern. Pulling along in the sludge like everything else on this dead sea. Out of boredom he leans to the side where there is a camera feed monitor. He looks, squints. Grabs the headset and puts it to his ears.

Please, whoever is out there, help us! We can hear you! Please, we need your—

Marhault throws the headphones down. Grabs the binoculars. Adjusts them. Nothing in the visible light spectrum. He begins to scan and roars a curse as infrared comes around.

†

"Captain! Captain!" Marhault's voice screeching over the radio catches Mellliagraunce's attention. The urgency of it. His fingers around the mic, squeezing.

"What?"

"Captain, there is someone outside the slaves' crate right now."

"One has escaped?"

"No, not Thovic, sir. It looks... I'm using the bino-scopes, Captain. Heat signature... it looks like some kind of stealth warrior."

Melligraunce narrows his eyes as he looks aft across his ship to where he can see Marhault's silhouette. Half an arm gone. All his quills.

From below, Uttar, one of his oldest, saltiest crewmen grumbles up to him. "That monastery was associated with a warrior religious order, sir. Aye, I know that much."

"They've come to my ship, eh?" Melligraunce listens intently. Nods. Uttar only speaks when he has something to say. A good captain knows when to listen. He raises the mic back to his mouth and says, "Agravain, get weapons to the stern on the double. We're being boarded."

†

Commander Lwanga turns on his active camo and emerges from the hatch. He sees Brother Becket outlined in his Visuals. Climbs up to him. Immediately his own universal translator kicks on, hears the pleading voices down below go from unintelligent murmurs to very clear begging.

"Have you spoken to them?" Lwanga asks.

"I've tried— they just," Becket huffs. "They're despondent. They won't listen. They're just begging and begging."

"Okay. Brother Thomas?"

From just below, under the open hatch, Thomas rogers up. "Yes sir?"

"You and Brother Scammacca get the FBW up here, put a hole in the side of this crate. Get these people down into the submersible." Even as he listens for an answer, Lwanga climbs to the top and searches for the other two crates. Making a plan.

"Yes, sir."

Lwanga turns to Becket. "I'm sending coordinates right now to the dropship. It's going to remote pilot this way. What we're going to have to do is—"

A muzzle roars to life from the stern of the Hhrothgar ship. Commander Lwanga explodes mid-sentence. Fragments of his armor, fritzing out and revealing themselves even as they rocket forth, mangled shards now. The sea round them pockmarked with debris.

Becket shoves himself down out of the line of fire. His own active camo fizzing like frying oil, glitching on and off from the shrapnel of Commander Lwanga peppering all over him.

The crate's shell comes alive with gunfire. layering it in spurts and ricocheting off, slapping welts into the sea's surface before being lost forever.

"Commander is down!" Becket says, engaging the shoulder-mounted mortars on his suit. The explosives pop off into the air several meters high and engage their rockets. Flinging towards the stern of the ship.

Becket looks over, sees the Commander's boots still maglocked to the shell of the crate. The Thovic inside screaming in absolute terror. The Hhrothgar enemy sends another explosive that strikes the crate, rings like a gong.

"These guys are using anti-vessel weapons against us! Our armor isn't—" more gunfire deafens him. Becket feels the crate shudder underneath him. Jerking like a giant hand is slapping at it. He hears the tow cable rachet begin to turn.

He looks around, feels the crate being pulled into the body of the ship. Closer to their guns.

Heavy Fire and Offerings to the Sea

"Everything has gone sideways!" Brother Becket shouts over the comms. He crosses himself, takes a deep breath. "Commander is in judgment now. Pray for his soul. Fight for ours. The enemy is engaging us with heavy munitions and towing in the slave crate towards the ship. All hands up above to engage in a firefight while Brothers Thomas and Scammacca proceed with the FBW. Move it!"

Becket maglocks around to the side of the crate and swings his rifle up. Because his suit's camo is glitching out, he must appear to them as some kind of mirage snapping in and out of focus. "Let 'em know me by the muzzle flash, then."

He opens fire.

Along the stern of the of the skeletal ship, a line of Hhrothgar crewmen is getting into place with the weaponry. Becket sends spat after spat of gunfire across the ever-narrowing gulf between them. Two crew drop immediately. They follow the shots and turn their attention on him.

"What's the mission parameters here?" Brother Bosco asks over the comms. "The Just War Theory?"

"We owe it to the captives to try and rescue them. Relics are secondary at best, now," Becket says.

"Roger."

Brothers Clotilde, Bosco and Magallenes burst out of the hatch and scramble up the crate. Guns out, they waste no time. Bosco's combat drones follow him up, swing out wide to the starboard and go high. Brother Scammacca emerges and braces himself over the hatch. Grabs at something and heaves up on an industrial cutting tool. Brother Thomas beneath it, shoving up.

They tilt the field breaching wheel—the FBW—and fire it up. The cutting tool on the end is a man-sized hole saw. They press it against the crate at the central bottom along the exterior wall facing the hatch.

Sparks fly. The crate's metal squeals. Immediately people inside begin to shout from the noise.

"This crate has just withstood explosives," Becket says. "It'll take a minute to cut through."

"Do we have that?" Scammacca asks.

"Not really," Becket says as he ducks from counterfire. "Thomas?"

"Yes?"

"Get the prisoners down below. We'll follow once they're in. If everything gets worse, get what you can and close the hatch. Detach from the crate. Move away. The dropship is coming in. Commander signaled it."

"What about you guys?"

An explosion rings off the top corner of the crate, tearing a chunk of metal off and raining sizzling fragments inside. The prisoners scream.

"Knights 15 13, brother. We'll do what we do." He leans back into the fight. "So much for extra sneaky. Let loose everything we've got. We need explosions on their side."

Clotilde and Magallenes fire off their shoulder-mounted mortars. Bosco starts to maneuver the combat drones into a strafing position. They begin making runs along the gunwales of the ship, taking potshots at the crew. Dropping a few here and there.

The lead drone fires a packet of consonance quattour or CQ4, a "tunable" demolitions device that uses sonics to create an explosion disproportionate to the size of the weapon. Tuning the explosive requires training, so the drones get equipped with pre-tuned blocks. The first one detonates three meters above the deck. Numerous crew fall, a head shorter after the explosion.

The drones start taking heavy fire and they scatter in evasive maneuvering. Potshots still snapping off, doing what they can.

"I don't want to sink it, not yet if we can help it," Becket says. "Clotilde, see if you can hit the rachet drawing us in. Buy us some time."

Clotilde fires his rail gun at it. The first shot punches a hole in the metal covering over the sprocket winching in the cable. He goes to fire again as a hail of return fire sprays around him. He rolls, maglocks to the side and ducks back.

The FBW's grinding sound changes in pitch, goes to a much higher note. Scammacca kills the power to it. The large circle they've cut out tilts outward as he removes the tool. He grabs it by the rim and shoves it off into the sea. "Breached."

Scammacca disables his active camo and leans into the hole. The briny stench of group sweat and being forced to stand in their own waste hit him. "Let's go!" he shouts as he offers his hand to the closest Thovic. A woman, battered and sweaty, greasy and dirty, wearing torn clothes. A sobering picture of what these people have been through in the last few days. A deep-seated fear in her eyes as if with such a violent shift in her life, she can trust nothing. Tears streaking down her face, she hesitates to take his hand. He rushes, trying not to scare her but knowing they have so little time. Pulls her out. Points down into the submersible's hatch.

The crackle of gunfire all around her frays her nerves even more than they are. But she steps out. Works her way down. Scammacca leads the next one down. "Thomas, get a line going to the hold. These folks have no idea about anything. See if you can look up their language—"

Another explosive hits. Dead center. More screams from inside. Pushing. Shoving. "Don't let anyone get trampled!" Becket shouts.

"I'm trying," Scammacca says, ushering them out.

Becket comes around the crate's corner. Looks up overhead, says, "Bosco, what are the drones seeing?"

Bosco says, "Looks to be about thirty crewmen left. Heavy artillery as you can see. I'm getting them— oh, they just shot one down. Okay, give me a sec—"

Another explosion rings off the starboard side of the crate. Clotilde scrambles up on top and out of the way and Magallenes swings around to the side.

"Bosco!" Magallenes shouts as something thuds into the sea on their side.

Becket races around, staying overhead from where Scammacca is pulling prisoners out. He sees an eerily still Bosco. On the Devil's Throat Sea, laying on his back, missing his right arm completely. Right leg at the knee. Left leg a little higher. Left arm at the elbow. His active camo so damaged it flickers with sparks. His vitals all flat on the display in Becket's Visuals.

As that ever-hungry body of bizarre liquid begins to lose viscosity around him, Becket watches Brother Bosco's corpse get swallowed, inch by inch. The crate tows closer to the ship, and down the Devil's Throat one man goes.

"Clotilde, draw a bead on what they're hitting us with."

"I've been trying." Clotilde lies prone on the crate's roof, dangerously open to enemy fire. Sighting on the target.

"Try harder." Becket looks back to the crate, climbs up to where he can see inside. Half empty. Only half. The barrage of fire from the ship continues. Small arms pebbling the metal surface, keeping them ducked down.

"Eyes on," Clotilde says and fires. A rail gun round from him chunks through the air at the speed of sound. It leaves a sizzling blue electrical trace where the air is electrified. Whatever he shot at explodes on the deck of the ship. The enemy scatters, shocked by the blast behind them.

"Got it," Clotilde says. He shoves backwards towards the edge of the roof over the back wall of the crate. As his feet dangle, he grabs the edge and pulls. Another barrage of return fire plinks off the metal. A separate, staccato blast follows it. Clotilde jerks. Stops.

Becket is within arm's reach. Sees his friend go motionless. Another explosion hits the crate high up. More screaming from inside; it begins to tune out and becomes just some other part of the background noise and loses its relevance now that those sounds belong to living people. God's people. God's people his friends are dying for. Becket grabs Clotilde by his waist and pulls down. The warrior collapses backwards. Held limp in one of Becket's arms, Clotilde stares up at the passing sky without a care. The face of his helmet shattered by a round, dead center.

"They got a sniper, too," Becket laments. He tugs off the rail gun and lowers Clotilde's body down to Scammacca who drops him into the hatch.

"Becket," Magallenes says.

"Yeah, go." Already three Knights down. They've been up here for a minute. "Oh, Lord, be with us," he says.

Magallenes says, "Just a head's up, they're shooting down the drones, too. After Bosco got hit, they just started station-keeping and, you know, they're sitting ducks."

"Let's get these prisoners out of here and we can worry about anything else."

"Roger."

Becket works his way around the side again, sees how little left they have to go. Enemy rounds start snapping to life around him and he backs up. He turns and says, "Listen, brothers. I think we can get these hostages. But we need to take a vote on whether or not to try for anything or anyone else. We've lost so much even since I wanted to press forward."

"Full frontal assault kits would be nicer than our light armor," Magallenes says.

"We don't have them," Becket says. "You want to go forward or fall back?"

No hesitation. "Go forward."

Scammecca says, "We should keep going. We're in it now. Besides, what do they want these hostages for? Anybody know?"

"Slaves, probably." Becket shrinks back as more rounds strike nearby. "The crew can see us, active camo or no."

"This is ugly," Magallenes says.

"Sure is." Becket checks his ammo. Grabs a grenade. "We gotta buy ourselves some time." He pulls its pin and chucks it at the aft end of the ship. It explodes near the already-damaged winch pulling them in. The cable rattles furiously and Becket can see the gearbox driving the winch tear open.

The cable severs, and falls limp into the sea.

Becket hears someone on the ship hollering invective. The crew scrambles.

"Fire at the cable!" Becket shouts. "Keep them from getting it!"

The Knights strafe the fluid and the tow cable. A crewmember nearly dives over the stern and grabs at the cable. He takes several rounds, but somehow attaches the cable to himself before he goes limp. Several of his compatriots scramble behind him, grabbing at him in any way they can. Pulling him back in. And with him, the tow cable.

Becket readies another grenade. "Just have to hit that crowd, maybe—" that staccato bark of the sniper snaps out of nowhere, hits Becket's rifle. Shatters it. Knocks the wind out of him. He stumbles back, drops the grenade. It slaps onto the surface of the sea and rolls on the shocked surface in one still moment of silence. As it settles against the surfaced area of the submersible, the trigger flicks and the countdown begins.

Five seconds and Becket throws himself down to the hatch. Reaches out.

Four seconds and his fingers slip along the surface of the explosive. Thumb and forefinger grabbing, the suction from the sea overpowering. It's half submerged. No going back now.

Three seconds and he stabs one finger onto it, shoves it in deeper, the tension of the explosive's timer playing against the careful need he has to push hard enough to get it down without pushing so hard the dilatant fluid becomes a solid against him.

Two seconds and he's down up to his shoulder, slides his arm back out. Swings off to the opposite side while rolling up and shouts, "Brace yourselves—"

The grenade explodes. Becket feels the submersible wrench under him. He's thrown forward, hits the crate with his face and chest. A bubble of hardened fluid forms and puffs out—physics of detonation fighting physics of viscosity reactions. A pinhole fizzes open at the surface. Like a tea kettle venting a furious line of steam, the power of the explosion eeks forward. A harsh sizzle.

"Oh, thank you, Lord—" Becket says and then the pinhole ruptures completely. Earthquake. The sea belches forth with a swirl of black smoke and angry flames. A sizeable plume of dilatant fluid flings into the air, the force of the blast making the globs compress into hardened, nightmarishly pointed shapes. If they hold that density when they rain back down. . .

"Anybody fall?" Becket asks with whatever breath he can muster. Even with his helmet on, the explosion was near enough to partially deafen him. A crack runs down his visor. The remaining Thovic are screaming. His remaining Knights are scrambling. "The fallout from— up above—"

Scammacca looks up and sees the incoming, crouches down around the hatch opening. Magallenes is still magbooted to the side of the crate, covers his head. Becket, down on the crate low enough for his toes to be in the sea, does the same.

The first glob hits the roof of the crate like a chunk of stone. Rings like a gong—a noise they're getting familiar with. The second glob crashes down, rings out. Scammacca makes a startled howl as a glob hits on his shoulder. A Thovic male pushes his way out the hole in the crate. Becket shouts and makes a *shooing* motion, but the male pays no mind.

A glob the shape of a stalactite hits him in the head. Digs in deep. The male shudders and goes stiff. Goes limp. Bits begin to pepper all around as he tilts over. The glob begins to liquify as his corpse collapses into the sea.

Another glob hits. Then another comes down, then a thousand. Raining about them. Everyone takes hard hits and then the skies clear like turning off a faucet.

Becket groans. He leans inside the submersible to view the damage. The interior wall of the vessel has an ugly indentation, but nothing more. The pinhole vent through the surface must have channeled enough of the explosion up.

"Where are we with this?" he asks as he climbs the side of the crate. His grenade disabled the ship's winch. The crew has formed a chain gang, a tug of war formation. They're hauling in the crate in heaves and spurts.

Motion on top of the nuclear drive catches his eye. Sunlight glinting off a barrel. Becket ducks as the report cracks out. A new chunk clinks and flies off the crate where his head was before.

"Knights, we've got a minute, tops. We've got to go."

Someone shouts over on the crew's side. Becket feels the tow cable go slack. "Why'd they let go?" He looks inside through one of the breathing vents. Sees the remaining few of the Thovic prisoners poised, ready for their turn to go out the hole and into safety.

A cough and roar. His instincts tell him RPG. The crate rocks violently as flames lick around the front of it, roll towards him. Inside the crate, the side facing the ship bows inward in slow motion as ripples in the metal flail outwards like they would on a pond.

The explosion bursts through and time speeds back up. The inside of the crate takes a burst of superhot air. Shock from the explosion. The Thovic coming out of the hole as the RPG hit knocks him floundering off the lip of the submersible. Face first into the Devil's Throat Sea. Five meters off the crate. His feet kick for a second as he tries to spin around. His arm wheels through the air and then goes away.

All of him does.

Becket shakes off the blast and looks back inside. The last male moves past him and rushes to the hatch. Becket scans quickly in disbelief of the damage wrought, darts his eyes away. "Alright. Praise God. We got everybody now."

The tow cable yanks, shudders the crate. Another cough, another roar. "Incoming!"

The crate rends in half all the way down to the flooring. There it rends upwards into a fold whose peak runs a line down the middle of the blasted thing. Moaning and a quiet, startled yelp come from inside. Survivor. Survivors? He just looked inside the crate. There was no one.

"I think there's somebody alive inside there," Scammacca says. He tries to lean in but they're waiting for him, zipping a line of fire through the split whenever he shows his head.

"I just looked—" another line of fire from the ship blasts through the ruined crate. Becket grabs Scammacca and pulls him back from returning fire from inside the crate. "Keep your melon outta there for a second," Becket says. "You're just drawing fire. We'll get back in—" another explosion. "Just. . ." he holds up a cautioning hand.

Scammacca hanging on the exterior of one side, Magallenes and Becket on the other. The crate's fold in the flooring tears, metal squealing and the towing action and resistance of the dilatant fluid fight. Two pieces spread out wide, blotches of fire along the walls. Still attached to the crate, the submersible shifts hard as well. The hatch draws off to one side and the newest Knight comes to the top.

"C'mon, brothers!" Thomas shouts, holding out an arm to Scammacca who is still two more arm's lengths away. Immediately gunfire rips through the shredded crate and around Thomas. He takes a round in the armor and ducks.

"Thomas, detach and dive. Detach and dive!"

"I'll come around and get you," Thomas says.

The three Knights on the surface spin towards the enemy and open fire. Thomas's reticent arm comes out of the hatch's opening, grabs the lid. Pulls it shut.

Under cover of gunfire, the Knights hear the submersible's magnet detach from the crate with a deep thump. The hatch sinks, and they keep firing. Four yards off the stern of the ship, surrounded in blood and flame.

In Good Hands and Poor Bargains

The crate wobbles under incredible stress and then with a final shriek, fully tears in half. The two sides begin to dip down, opening like a book. Their exterior walls plunging towards the sea, the interior walls with all their evidence of violence inside, opening to the sky.

"Use your KERS," Brother Becket says as he drops off the exterior and slams his feet onto the sea surface. The kinetic effect reception systems roll that energy up his legs into a battery/capacitor combo on his back, storing it. The natural resistance of the sea keeps him afloat, and with every step he stomps. The Devil's Throat Sea under his feet splatters and forms a rippling disc for him to stand on as he rushes off in a wide reversing arc to get the starboard side crate between him and the enemy.

Brother Magallanes follows, and Brother Scammacca races around the opposite way. Gunfire punch holes into the paths behind them. An explosion kicks up a gout of hardening fluid globs near Becket and Magallanes.

"We've got to scan for snipers, somebody using some kind of vision to see us under active camo," Magallanes says. As he does, a sniper's round careens past his head, so close the way it slices through the air like a knife in his ear.

"And fast," Scammacca says. He reaches the crate on the far starboard side and jumps up on it, magbooting to the rear end of it. Becket and Magallanes do the same behind him, all unscathed.

They watch the remains of the prisoner crate haul up the aft gunwale. Two crewmen lean into it and carefully board. Searching through the remains.

The other two crates jitter and yank one good time each. The Knights hear the now-familiar clanking of the winches towing the crates in.

†

Brother Thomas doesn't know the first thing about how to pilot the submersible. He stares at the control console for a moment, trying to remember the one-minute rundown Commander Lwanga—God, grant eternal rest unto him and let perpetual light shine upon him—gave them all. At the time it seemed more of a general *here's everything you'll never need to know* kind-of thing to fill up the time between boarding and mission.

Now, Thomas's eyes fall on the joysticks, saying, "Okay. That one on the left is the pitch. . . no. . . the yaw. . . or, no. It's the pitch. That one *there* is the yaw. And then that is. . ." Colorful buttons, dials. "That's the depth gauge. Even I know that one. And that's the. . . the ballast read-out? No, it's the pitch percentage— oh. Blast it, I don't. . ."

He turns around behind him, and one compartment aft the throng of shivering, scared and displaced Thovic begins. Men, women and children, battered. Stinking. Hungry, deprived. Consumed with dread.

Thomas turns back around. The tug of his brothers in battle up above him, calling. "They need my gun added to the mix. They need more—" his thoughts drift to Clotilde's corpse as Scammacca handed him down the hatch. They're losing guns pretty fast up there.

The radio burps with a noise of static. One of his brothers keying up and letting go, maybe. The reception under the sea was terrible, anyways. A welcome distraction from the gravity of his ignorance in the controls. But when the moment is gone, the frustration of it all swells up tenfold. One of the Thovic women who has been weeping, snorts and groans. Coughs. The murmur with her seems to grow, even if only in Thomas's ears.

"I'm in over my head. Literally and figuratively." He takes a deep breath. Then another. Closes his eyes. Makes the sign of the cross over himself. Prays to his patron saint.

"Apostle Thomas called Didymus, I pray you intercede on my behalf before our blessed Savior, through Whom all things are possible. Please help me in this moment of need, the same way you always have for me, your fellow twin. Through the love and mercy of Jesus Christ, all glory and honor to Him. In the name of the Father, and of the Son, and of the Holy Spirit—"

"Excuse me?" from behind. Through his universal translator, Thomas hears the words a split second after they're spoken in the sandpaper-grit of the Thovic male voice.

"—amen." Thomas says and turns around, trying not to look defeated. Drowning. The Thovic man has leaned into the controls compartment, hope on his wide-eyed face. The dried blood and the numerous cuts along his cheek and lip seem forgotten to him.

"I come to tell you, I am a pilot of these things," he says and points a finger at the controls. "You look all the same way I did when I first took the position to, as you know, drive these."

"You—" Thomas hears Becket in his head. *And anyways, we're in good hands with our Lord. If you can't shoulder the burden by yourself, He will help you.* "—you are a pilot for this type of submersible? This, right here? You're a pilot... for these?"

The Thovic shrugs. "Same brand, yes. Same controls. Bigger in size, our submersibles, mostly is what I drive. Bigger. But all the same. Built by the same hands." He waves his own hands around, encompassing the world. "We troll the sea, right? Lots get lost down here, you know it. So, yes. Yes, I am a pilot. The pilot, yes." He laughs, points at Thomas. "You look all the same way I did. It funny to me."

And anyways, we're in good hands with our Lord. If you can't shoulder the burden by yourself, He will help you. I've learned that time and time again.

Thomas smiles as joy overwhelms him and holds his rosary to his lips. Kisses the crucified man on it. He beams, "Well, amen to that."

†

"It's pretty straight forward, really," Brother Magallanes says, "There's not a whole lot of places a sniper could be."

"High up," Brother Becket says. "This whole thing is some skeleton and a barge hull. No masts, no lookout, no crow's nest."

"Comms tower coming off the nuclear drive," Brother Scammacca says. He peeks around the crate and endures a spat of gunfire as he looks upwards. Ducks back behind. "Tower is a no-go, all flimsy antennas. But... I think at the base of it there's somebody."

Becket darts out and back in. The drive is essentially a large box on the aft end, jabbed on deck between the iliac crests of the ancient lizard hip bone. The top of it is equivalent to a small roof. A man lying on his belly, the spill of quills like a waterfall down his shoulder as he rests his cheek on a rifle. Obscured just enough by the features of the drive. "Confirmed, sniper on the nuclear drive."

Scammacca moves around the crate to the other side. "Cover me for just a second."

Becket and Magallanes share a countdown through their Visuals and both swing out at once, strafing fire along the stern of the ship. Scammacca takes another look and drops a waypoint on the sniper's position in his Visuals. Ducks back in and a suit-mounted mortar pops off up into the air. They're designed to fling about fifteen meters into the air on a directionless *poof* of propellant, and then an on-board aiming computer corrects its orientation and activates a rocket, zeroing in on the intended target at over thirty meters per second.

As return fire flings all along the crates, the mortar reaches its zenith and corrects, fires its rocket. Hurls back down to the ship and the Knights hear the explosion from behind the crates. See a quick plume of smoke unfurl.

"Sounds like a bull's eye to me," Scammacca says.

"Gotta confirm the hit was good, though," Becket says. "Hold on."

He chances another sneak peek and sees smoke still rising from where the sniper was. Starts to duck back behind cover and sees two crewmen on the ruined slave crate dragging out a female Thovic. She's injured, still kicking and twisting at her waist in some vain form of struggle.

"They've got a live prisoner," Becket says. "Someone who survived inside the crate this whole time."

"I doubt we can do anything," Magallanes says. "Not just yet anyways. When the dropship shows up—"

"Knights!" a voice bellowing over the loudspeaker, crawling through their universal translators. It's not until then that Becket realizes how quiet the fight has gotten. "I have a bargain."

Silence has descended. Only the muddy undulating sounds of the dilatant fluid seeping along, the resonating hum of the nuclear drive forever turning and turning. The slap of the lizard's paddled feet striking. The winches turning, drawing them ever closer. But no gunshots.

Becket shrugs. He switches his helmet speakers to translate his speech to the Hhrothgar tongue. "What?" he shouts.

†

Captain Melligrance stands with the stolen skull in hand, listening to the wind as it howls ever so quietly inside the eye sockets. Mic in his hand, he looks down to the Thovic woman, collapsed next to him. Her head drawn back by Agravain's fistful of her hair. Not quite the Hhrothgar quill, but a cousin to it.

The captain sees a look of distaste on his first mate's face. Holding the hostage like that. Trying to force himself to have the iron will needed to work for Captain Melligrance. Trying and failing. Pathetic. Agravain pays no attention to his captain. He is focused on the skull in Melligrance's hand. Twisting his head as if he is listening to something. The dry wind blowing in its sockets.

The captain glares at Agravain. "Head in the game," he says. "Or your head will be in the chopping block." Agravain snaps out of whatever he is thinking, eyes locking with the captain.

"Always," he says, then looks back to the woman.

She still weeps. Still drawing quick, gasping breaths. The blood from her nose and mouth—maybe hers, maybe from the slaughter inside the crate when the captain decided it was too far compromised to bother with anymore—along her face.

"You are extra freight on my ship," the captain says to the woman. "Not my catch, not my sell. I have already been paid to haul you to port by my friend and his ship. This . . . this will cost him a fortune. Your friends over there . . . if you were my catch, I would be incensed beyond comparison. Even so, this is a black mark on my reputation. And for what? You? Your friends?"

He looks to the skull. "*This?*" Melligrance looks at her, shows her the skull. "See this? They worship this, you know. Your almost-rescuers, worship dead bones of an alien species to them."

She looks but her lips quiver too much to form words.

"What think you, if they would accept this relic but would leave you to my devices?" She says nothing. He squats down, leans in. "Because I believe they will. And that serves me fine."

Captain Melligrance takes her by the chin and twists her bruised face to meet his. She tries to avoid eye contact but in a moment, it dawns on her that eye contact is the only way she'll be freed from this particularly harsh grip, she reticently gives it.

The captain smiles. "Good. I would like to keep you. My men are lonely." She gasps and looks away. He can tell by her dress, the jewelry in her hair, how soft she is, she came from comfort. And now, she will never know it again. "And when they are full of you, in your new cage you will go. With fresh grass and some bread, of course. We want you around for quite some time." He laughs and stands up.

"Because they will get lonely again. And again."

A voice from behind the crates calls again. "What?"

Captain Melligrance holds the mic to his mouth. "Where is your back-up? Why were we not stormed, fore and aft, overrun with the might of your God's greatest warriors?"

"Don't worry. We're giving you the chance to surrender."

The captain laughs. He makes sure to heave his guffaws across the remaining sea and over the slowly approaching crates. Even though he can still smell the heat and burning propellants that made short work of Seneschal, his sniper, he finds mirth in the comment.

"Your foolishness is good for my morale, Knight. I will give you that you are entertaining, if not delusional. See what I have here?" He holds the skull up high, slowly twisting it in the breeze to draw the eye. "Fear not, my crew is well-disciplined and will not fire upon you. Now, look."

He waits a moment and sees a single head peek around one of the crates. He hears murmurs from his remaining crew that he takes to mean they've seen heads as well. "Agravain, how many did you see?"

His first mate looks startled by the question. Wide eyed, he swallows. Looks here and there. The captain smiles and snarls all at the same time. "Leave her. Get a count from the sailors all around you worth their salt." Agravain does.

"You seek this, Knights. The object of your worship. I possess it, and even now it preaches to me as the wind whirls and whooshes through its empty cavities. I have come to be fascinated by it, certainly. But I am also a businessman, a merchant, a leader. . . and you have cost me considerably."

"You trade in violence. That's no business worth doing."

"It is the only business you and I have. We have both paid in blood up to this point, and to be candid, I'll need the crew I have left just to moor my ship up when we reach a berth. By the stars, I've lost my best machinist mate and two cooks in this little riot of yours. But, to the skull here. Do you wish it returned to you?"

"We're here for everything stolen from the monastery, and the woman," comes the voice from behind the crate.

"How gluttonous of you, Knight. Something I thought you were taught to avoid. But no. Pick one. The skull or the woman."

"No."

"That is the bargain," the captain says, as if he is offering two things of equal value, both of which are costing him more to give away than to retain. "I will bestow upon you one or the other in exchange for peace. You can, without fear of betrayal, receive one into your very hands, and then depart my sight without further having to commit your corpses to being swallowed by the aptly named Devil's Throat underneath us."

"And if I turn you down?"

"Then this, I suppose," Captain Melligrance huffs and hands the mic to Marhault the stern watch. He grabs the woman, and her shrieks carry further than the captain's laugher ever could. He shoves her to the very edge of the stern, holding her with one arm. He holds the skull out with the other. Turns to Marhault and says, "Tell them I said this: one will go in the drink, and the other will bear witness as I finish killing them."

Marhault nods and clears his throat. "The captain says he will drop either the skull or the woman into the sea and the other will watch as—"

"I said *bear witness.*"

"—uh, the other— the other will *bear witness* as he kills the lot of you."

"Tell them they are out of time."

"Time is almost up—"

Melligrance roars. Marhault stiffens completely, then clears his throat again. "You are out of time now."

"And you are no better than that idiot first mate of mine," Melligrance says with a heavy note of disdain.

Marhault goes to set down the mic, but the captain turns to him. His glare lets the stern watch know to stay where he is.

Agravain runs up to the captain and whispers in his ear, something about probably four Knights behind the crates. The captain nods. Two crewmen sneak to the aft corners of the ship. They have devices like wheels with slapping paddles instead of a tire around them. In the center of each is a short-barreled gun. They wind up the wheel paddles and set them on the fluid. The paddles begin spinning, slapping the sea surface and racing to flank the approaching crates.

The captain looks back at Marhault and says, "What will it be?"

Marhault groans and puts the mic back up to his lips. "Well? What will it—" his ritualistically shaved head kicks back with the impact from a gunshot. The remaining crew on the stern roar and open fire as a fresh sweep of bullets flies across them.

Captain Melligrance turns his head just as a round skims past his forehead. A second shot dead center mass into his armor knocks him back and he loses his grip on the woman. She crumples, paralyzed by fear. The wheel paddles get to the crates, begin firing as they pass behind them.

From behind the crates, the three Knights in active camo rush out. Their Ceramatex armor taking the wheel paddles shots, but glitching and getting damaged all the same. Their KERS stomping transferring energy in every slap into the sea as they cover the distance between them and the stern. Brazenly marauding onto the ship.

The Hard Push and the Associated Costs

"You should have shot the guy holding the woman and the skull," Brother Scammacca says as he comes up on the stern and jumps, lands on the deck. Keeps firing.

"He'd have dropped them both into the sea," Brother Becket says, coming around his side and getting on board. "Brother Thomas, where are you?"

The comms crackle like frying bacon, but the transmissions work. "Surfacing in just a few meters."

"Be ready," Becket says. Scammacca and Brother Magallanes rush to the starboard, Scammacca slowing down at he nears the centerline stern where the woman and skull lay. Magallanes pushes forward, towards the wing. Becket does the same on the port side, spats of gunfire as they try to scatter and drop the crew.

The hard push, Becket called it as that maniac was setting the bargain in place over the loudspeaker. "It's not really a winning solution. But our back is against the wall here. No back-up, heavy losses, outgunned, hostages, everything. It's desperate, might as well make it ugly too." They all shrugged and agreed.

The hard push it is.

Scammacca jumps over the corpse of the bald crewman pegged between the eyes moments ago. Sees the crumpled Thovic woman, sobbing with her face in her hands. Sees the hatch of the submersible shove away the dilatant fluid of the surface of the sea, breaching like some underwater predator.

No skull. No leader threatening woman or relic.

"Get forward and below decks!" Becket shouts at Scammacca and Magallanes. "I'll keep their attention here. You see if we can sink this pig."

Becket dodges around a crest of bone protruding from the deck, ducking as rounds take chunks out of it. His active camouflage is fritzing, but at worst he's still translucent. Pinning him down is hard.

"Is he serious?" Scammacca asks. His own active camo mostly intact except for two rounds he took earlier.

Magallanes nods, still untouched. "He always is in a firefight."

†

Captain Melligrance watches as Agravain fires at the invaders. He studies as the first mate stays behind cover, dipping around the side or top and wildly fire two or three rounds. No looking where he is shooting. Certainly no aiming.

"Agravain," he calls out. The first mate turns, sees his captain staring intently at him from only a few meters away.

"Captain?"

"I thought you spent time in the military, did you not?"

"Aye, skipper. I did."

"Rifleman, you said?"

"Aye, skipper."

"Then why the potshots and wasted efforts?"

Agravain cannot help but look as though he's been caught in a lie. "Well, skipper, this isn't much of a rifle, you see," he holds up his handgun, turning this way and that as if to show off just how different it is.

"I see," the captain says. "Completely different gun, completely different competency."

"As embarrassed as I am to say, yes."

The captain scowls. "You're a liar."

"What? No, skipper—"

"I verified your military time. You hold records for shooting. This here," he wags a hand at Agravain and his surrounds, "this is nothing more than cowardice. Throwing' your shots every which way but to the enemy. You might as well just tell me you're siding with them."

"Never, skipper!"

The captain nods gravely, and the motion silences the first mate. "From trained sharpshooter to commercial sailor to me, a failure and a liability."

"My captain, I—"

The captain lazily aims his gun in Agravain's direction. "We'll have words, Agravain. We will, I swear it. Until then, you better earn me not shooting you in the back. Because you're doing it to me right now."

†

The two Knights send volleys of return fire forward down the ship's midline. Brother Magallanes says, "I'll go port, you go starboard. KERS to the front. I saw open decking on the bow. We can enter there."

"Roger that." Brother Scammacca stands and rushes to the gunnel, firing one burst at a crewman chasing him with automatic fire. He jumps over the railing and slams into the Devil's Throat Sea. The dilatant fluid tremors in a radius around his feet, solidifying under the impact. The Kinetic Effect Receptor System begins to cycle.

He channels his stored kinetic energy down through his legs, pounding the sea with every footfall as he races forward. The KERS transfers the energy outward, hammering the non-Newtonian fluid into its unique physics effect.

One hand on the freeboard surface of the boat, he runs alongside it. Staying this close to the skin of the ship, he hopes anyone above taking shots at him will have too hard a time leaning over to do any meaningful damage.

Magallanes races to his own side, bullets whizzing past. A small explosion blasts forth behind him, helping to propel him overboard. He rolls, his feet striking the sea. The bizarre disc of rigid fluid forms under him. But pursuing fire kicks up around him, creating their own miniature versions of that effect.

Magallanes races forward, being astounded by God's unlimited creativity even in the middle of the firefight. The sea reacts as the bullets meant for him punch it, and Magallanes sees little flattened projectiles ride the surface of the sea for a moment before the fluid loosens and flows, swallowing them one by one. With his active camo still working, he's little more than a transparent silhouette making circular splash patterns on the sand-colored sea.

Quick flaming eruptions up above from muzzle flashes. Like fireworks in the sky. Magallanes squeezes off two potshots and keeps his eye on the front of the ship. The strafing fire dies off the further he gets, invisibly lost to their unaided gaze.

He makes it to the bow and sees Scammacca round his side. They both look up above while running—to stop is to be drawn below—and they see openings in the freeboard under the bow. Like windows large enough for vehicles to enter. Certainly big enough for men.

They stomp harder, build up their KERS and then both leap up off the surface. They cannonball inside the mouth of the ship, hit the deck and roll into the belly.

†

"Brother Thomas, you read me?" Brother Becket asks as he darts around a small part of what little superstructure the bone ship has. Gunfire peppers every surface he's near; his active camouflage is glitching, but a quasi-invisible target is still harder to hit when it's moving. Distortions of the surface textures coupled with small electrical current spasms give his position away. The Hhrothgar crewmen still have to trace him, and so far, they're one step behind.

"Yes, I can hear you," Thomas's anxious and distorted voice comes back.

"I'm trying to get the last survivor up here," Becket pauses against a dark backdrop as two crewmen come racing around the corner. They're carrying a device that has two clamps on the front with a coil of copper and a trigger in the rear. Trying to short out his suit? Just a different weapon to try and kill him with?

Becket prays to his patron saint that his suit not glitch as they come near. And it does not. He whispers a prayer of thanks to the Lord for His kindness, lets the crewmen pass and then fires. As they collapse, they drop the device. He grabs it and examines it. Ducks back into a corner as three more crewmen come around.

One says, "He killed Barth and Grab'bhah. Where is the Vhor?"

Another spits and demands, "They brought a Vhor up here? For what?"

"It will light him on fire, that's for what, fool." The third says as he rolls over the bodies of their fallen mates. He takes a trinket off one and pockets it. Then stands and kicks at the corpse.

Becket sees the behavior and it only bolsters what he thinks of these savages. *Even in battle they disrespect and thieve from one another.*

The one who spat says, "It jumps dead batteries; it does not start fires!"

"This one is modified to severely scorch. To flesh, it will teach a harsh lesson. I've used it in the harem before on disobedient—"

Becket fires the Vhor at the at one of the dead bodies and lets go. It thuds heavily on the deck. The clamps spring forward on compressed gouts of gas, unspooling cables trailing back to the copper coil. Like a pulsed lightning bolt, the weaponized battery jumper sizzles sharply and then fire erupts from the body. The crewmen jump, get gunned down and Becket goes on the move.

"That was something different," he says.

"Becket? Were you hailing me?" Thomas comes over the comms again. Snaps Becket back to his plan.

"Yes, I need you to be ready to surface," Becket says as he lets the Vhor's spectacle draw the attention of the other crewmen. They leave the Thovic woman unguarded and rush to the new fire. "I'm getting the woman now."

"Copy, I'll come up on the port rear quarter."

"It's a plan." Becket leaps from a shadow onto the noonday-lit deck. The boat is its own spectacle of nearly nightmarish qualities. The fact it is built into a dead lizard the size of a vessel in its own right. Crewed by men that trade in bloodlust and savagery.

The fact he is in broad daylight only serves to make it more uncomfortable in a way. No lengthy shadows to hide the horrors. They're right out in the open.

He sees the woman and breaks off at a sprint for her. Ten meters and the gap will be closed. What crew are still running around are either not seeing him or are too good at acting like they are not to be the same pirates he was just fighting.

Twenty meters and he can hear her sobs, see the way her crown-to-chin length ears wobble with every hitch of her chest. Ten meters and she looks up. He knows she can make out his translucent smudgy form. Rescue has arrived.

Whoomph. An explosion at his side punches into his gut. His armor fritzes terribly as he's rocked off his feet and slams down onto the deck several meters back. He rolls and coughs hard, can taste blood in his mouth. "That's gonna leave a mark," he says. Gets to his feet as a second *whoomph* pops into life in the distance. He leaps as another explosion blossoms out where he just was. It kicks him from behind and he lands. He can't fight the momentum that shoves him forward. He flops uncontrollably along the deck. Stops himself and scrambles to his feet.

His Visuals flash red and starts displaying his newest injuries. He's going to need a medpod for what that explosion just did. All his vitals are suffering. A hit dead-on would have been the end of it.

He hears a commanding voice shout, "There! Off the port quarter! Let them have our wrath!" Becket turns and sees Thomas has surfaced. The exposed portion of the submersible is riddled in gunfire. He clicks over to his comms, says, "Thomas, dive. I don' have her and they're trying to breach the hull."

'Roger. I'm— I'm okay. We're going," he says through static. The hatch sinks and is swallowed by the sea. Becket coughs again and a single spat of gunfire drives him back. He finds a spot behind the reactor and huddles in.

His shoulder bumps into a ladder that reaches to the top of it, and he grabs hold.

†

"Same deal going aft," Brother Magallanes says. "You got starboard, I got port." The forward chamber they are in is a small boat launch. Two open skiffs are up on wenches. Nothing more than landing craft which look more like personal fishing craft than anything. Long canoes with flat planks for bench seating. A standing helm at the rear with an outboard motor assembly.

One is missing several panels along its bottom. Open to the sea. The Knights must have interrupted a major overhaul on the second one; the motor and helming controls have been removed and parts scattered all along a workbench. It too is missing its foremost floor panel.

"Those are no use to us," Brother Scammacca says as he runs by. He shouts over his shoulder, "Stay in contact," and disappears down a narrow passageway on the starboard side.

"Will do," Magallanes says and moves down his passageway.

Scammacca's voice crackles as it transmits through the ship's material, "Right off the bat, I've got forward berthing."

"Me too," Magallanes says. He shoves into the first hatch and sees a cramped space of swirled blankets on the floor, stippled with overstuffed pillows that might be beds for Hhrothgar children.

"They must huddle at night like puppies," Scammacca says. "Nothing but giant blankets and pillows so big six sailors can share one."

"Same here. No occupants."

"Moving out," Scammacca says. Magallanes does the same, adopting a mirroring pattern to his brother, the best he can. "More berthing," he says as he comes up to the next space.

"Me too. Mine looks like the captain's," Scammacca says. He flows into the space and sees three smaller pillows with adjoining blankets. A single piece of furniture that might be a dresser. A standing wardrobe as well. "Yeah, officer's quarters. Looks like he shares them, too."

Magallanes says, "Mine is more of the same. Crew berthing."

"We've got to get under the reactor. Moving out."

Both Knights flow down the passageway. Along the centerline sides of both passageways there are placards mounted over various small accesses. Magallanes uses his Visuals to translate the words stamped into them from the Hhrothgar language.

"Buoyancy chamber," Magallanes reads. "Lots of buoyancy chambers in this thing."

"Got to stay afloat in this muck outside," Scammacca says. "I bet you those take up most of the belly of the ship. That and the propulsion system."

"Makes sense."

"Let's breach these, then."

Magallanes sticks a wad of CQ4 onto the chamber hatch, which appears much too armored to take apart in a hurry. "Hopefully that will do something."

On the other side, Scammacca says, "Hopefully no one finds it before we blow it. They put all their metal into these chambers. It's impressively thick."

"That it is. Keep on, friend." They push aft, guns leading the way.

Magallanes travels a few meters and comes up on a ladder well leading up to the main deck. "Scammacca," he says. "Do you have a ladder well near you?" He transmits a photo of the one he's looking at over his Visuals.

"Looks like stairs to me. But yes, I'm got one right here with me."

"Naval term for stairs, goofball. Let's weld these doors shut real quick. Keep out any surprises."

Scammacca starts tack-welding along the door's seam. "I was starting to wonder why they haven't come down here yet."

"Maybe Brother Becket is keeping them busy. Maybe they're coming down another ladder well. Maybe—"

"Maybe they thought we bailed altogether," Scammacca says and puts away his welder. "Done, by the way."

Magallanes finishes two more welds and says, "I've been done for a while. Waiting on you."

"Liar."

"Whatever." They press aft again. They pass by the cramped mess hall on Scammacca's side. Magallanes passes by the armory, hastily emptied when word of the Knights 1513 came down the pipe.

Magallanes sees his passageway terminating up ahead as the clanking and droning of machinery gets louder. A side passageway splits off to his side, heading starboard. He clears it, sees Scammacca doing the same at the other end. "Clear," Magallanes says.

"Clear." Scammacca looks back to his original passageway, flicks his head. "Engine room door."

"On the way."

†

As soon as Brother Becket reaches the top of the reactor gunfire erupts below. The base of the ladder is struck several times and the metal warps, bends. Two rungs snap off and rounds ricochet all about. Becket rolls himself over the top of it and hunkers down against the flooring, which hums intensely with the power below. On the other side of the lip, stray gunfire still speckles in concussive blasts.

"I saw him there!" One of the Hhrothgar says as the shooting ceases. Other voices quibble with him and footfalls run around the reactor. Searching.

"OvRovid? OvRovid!" a voice from down below calls loudly. It dawns on Becket that the voice called loud enough to be heard on top of the reactor. He turns and sees a Hhrothgar come his way, oblivious to his presence.

"What?" The crewman named OvRovid calls down.

"Did you see the boarder come about the reactor?"

"No, don't you think I would have killed him if I had?"

"Well, look! He's about!"

OvRovid snickers derisively at the man down below and begins to walk the reactor's edge, gun ready. He gets halfway down the structure and has to step around the ruined remains of the sniper the Knights shot earlier.

"I'm glad you missed me when I was down there earlier," Becket says quietly. "These guys are cruel and rash. Violent. But not a trained, cohesive fighting force. We've got that going for us."

OvRovid is armed with a rifle whose barrel is easily a meter and a half long and equipped with a scope so long and blocky it looks like a stylized brick. Perfect for distance shooting. "Don't think he's going to be too wieldy with that thing in close quarters," Becket mumbles. "I could probably pick off some bad guys from up here. Cover fire."

Becket waits as OvRovid makes his round about the reactor top. As he reaches near enough, Becket springs out, gun forward. OvRovid whips the rifle up on point and its barrel hits Becket's gun, knocks it off target. His burst goes wild and the Hhrothgar swings with the butt of the rifle.

Becket's head knocks over hard but he moves with the force of it. Drops down in a push-up position the Takayama style calls P31, prone prayer position 1. From there he can twist and roll, stay put and deliver strikes and kicks. Even some takedowns and locks.

Becket rolls to one side and sweeps with his upper leg. Hammers OvRovid's knee from the side. The Hrothgar buckles but does not fall. He brings the awkward rifle around. Becket transitions to catch the muzzle and twists it. Rolls it around in his opponent's hand. Hooks it behind the knee and yanks the butt stock into the front of OvRovid's other shin. Push on the shin, pull on the back of the knee.

OvRovid collapses. Becket throws a knifehand strike, fingers straight and thumb indexed along the hand. The outside edge of his hand chops like an axe across OvRovid's face. "Aiming for your nose, but oh well," Becket says as he twists and hurls an elbow. That connects with OvRovid's jaw.

Lights out.

Becket untangles himself from the enemy, brusquely wiggles the long rifle free from his legs. As he checks to make sure it's armed, the Hhrothgar forcefully shoves up with a knife aimed for Becket's throat.

Becket throws both hands open, one hitting the inside of OvRovid's elbow and the other driving the knife up and away. The move is explosive. His arm bends all the way over under the overwhelming strike from Becket. The knife tip plunges into OvRovid's eye and he rolls over twitching.

Becket gets the rifle and ejects the magazine. Sees it only has two rounds left. He pats OvRovid down, looking for more. None to be found. He rechambers what he has and gets his own weapon, pauses in a crouch to gather his wits. Breathe. Say a Hail Mary.

"OvRovid!" from down below. "Come here."

Becket rolls his head on his neck and crouch-walks over to the edge of the reactor. Listens to the sounds. He brings the rifle up and steadies the muzzle on the lip of metal ringing the reactor, canted high into the air.

The voice from below calls for OvRovid again and Becket tips the barrel down, stands up in a rocketing motion, gun snug into his shoulder. Three Hhrothgar below. He fires twice and moves to the side as return fire comes. He throws the rifle like a spear at the other crewman and jumps off, following it down.

The rifle jabs the crewman, shoving him back. Becket lands on him, kicking him several meters back. The Hhrothgar roars impotently as he slips and falls off the back deck and into the sea. Becket does not waste time.

"Thomas, you got me?"

"Yes, brother. Tell me when."

Becket peers around the reactor's corner and sees the woman. He shrugs. "Might as well be now. Be ready."

†

The engine room is hot and so damp rivulets of moisture run freely down the blocky metal walls. With the reactor up on the deck, the gearing system it powers spins before the Knights.

"That one gear alone must weigh three tons if it's an ounce," Brother Scammacca says, looking at the drive shaft's gearing adornments.

The room is so full of machinery any free movement is impeded. A giant gearing box sits on both sides of it, one port and the other starboard. Huge radial bearing systems like concentric circles stand on end up against the outer walls. Giant femoral bone sockets pass through the wall, through the bearing ring and into metal shafts affixed to them. The shafts enter the gearing box. Drive shafts extend from the boxes, into a much larger gearing box that descends from the overhead. And above it, on deck, is the reactor.

Numerous other things become obstacles inside as well. A stack of flat battery packs and their associated cables and electronics. A curving system of steam piping that gorgeously wraps this way and that, several pipes shimmying as one around the room. The stink of burnt oil. Darkened stains from where it spilled. Globs of grease on the floor, runners of it squeezed out from bearing seals.

Brother Magallanes pulls out a block of CQ4 and starts examining the system. "Universal joint, differential, yadda yadda. . . forget it." He climbs to the top of the main gearbox under the reactor. "I'm putting it right here."

"Get it done already. We've got go."

Magallanes groans with some effort, says, "One second. . ." He then drops down and claps his hands. "Done. Let's get gone."

"Up forward in the mess hall, there's more open windows. We can drop down and make our way aft. Get everybody."

Magallanes says, "I like that idea," and moves out of the room, glad to shed the sweltering moist heat of that one space. Starts running.

"When are you going to blow it?"

"When Brother Becket says to." Magallanes says over his shoulder. "And preferably when we're not on board anymore."

Scammacca thinks about it for a second, nods. "Now then, I like that idea."

†

Brother Becket sweeps a line of gunfire around the cover he's behind and dodges return fire. Brothers Scammacca and Magallanes come barreling over the gunnel and back onto the deck. "Becket!" Magallanes shouts. "We've got the reactor's drive train rigged to blow. Just got to get off here now."

"Copy that," Becket says. "I'm still trying to get to the Thovic woman we saw."

"I'm near her," Scammacca says as he scans around, gunfire snapping about him. He ducks and rushes towards the woman. In the sea, the surfaced hatch flings open. Thomas clambers up, squats on the watertight rim and leaps to the stern.

He lands and stumbles forward, turning that motion into a run. He sees Scammacca coming over to him, pointing. Scammacca motions to the woman, says, "Thomas! We need to get her—" and with a high whistling sound he explodes in a mist of wet red and metal shrapnel. Thomas reflexively ducks as the blast pushes his way before dotting the sea behind them with Scammacca's ruins.

The Thovic woman screams, and Thomas stays low, moves to her. Fighting back his horror. He follows the trail of propulsion smoke from where Scammacca was hit forward. There, a deck feature, large enough to conceal a Hhrothgar with a rocket launcher.

"Scammacca! He's— he's gone! They just—" Thomas says as he reaches the woman. He takes her, the wilds of battle making his heart race. She screams and fights against him. He pulls and she kicks without any real aim, but the blows land about his head and shoulders anyway.

Becket comes over the comms. "I saw, Thomas. Do what you can to get her to the sub and Mags and I will—" a new spat of gunfire and a second explosion cut him off. Thomas can hear the barrage without needing the comms.

"Let me help you," Thomas says. He takes the woman with both hands and drags her backwards. She fights still, but her desolation overwhelms her. Her energy dries up and she finally begins crying even though she has precious few tears left.

They make their way to the stern where one of the Thovic men is waiting just below the lip of the hatch. "Hey!" he calls, and the man pops his head up.

Thomas has her and rears back to toss her when a zipping line of gunfire draw across him. It chews up knots of the deck with it, sending splinters and hot bits everywhere. He chucks the woman overboard. She hits the hatch and the man grabs her. It is a flawed thing, sloppy and ungainly, but she makes it and he pulls her down.

"She's aboard," Thomas says as he dodges from a second volley of gunfire. A third comes around, and as he moves he becomes conscious of being herded away from escape. He fires anyway, as crewmen pop up and shoot, then move behind cover as the next crewman takes over.

He sees Becket and Magallanes crossing inside, close quarters fighting as they drop one combatant at a time. Thomas turns to move one way and the high whistling sound pierces the air. Thomas drops to the deck. An explosion bursts just past him. Even from where he is he hears the Thovic man in the submersible hatch holler with alarm. He sees out his peripheral vision as the hatch flaps shut. Lowers below the sea.

"We're cut off," Thomas says. "The sub just dove under." He stands to race towards better cover and another zipping line of chasing gunfire sweeps at him. He feels the impacts along his legs and fire inside his veins lights up his entire world.

†

Brother Becket sees a crewman moving steady and fast, gun up in his shoulder. Becket lets a three round volley loose and the crewman spins on him just in time to take the rounds full on. He collapses.

"Brother Magallanes, we gotta push back to the stern. These guys just keep popping up, two for every one that drops."

"I was really hoping this guy was serious about not having hardly any crew left."

"I'm pretty sure he's a liar."

"No. . ."

Both Knights begin moving aft, cautious of whoever is firing rockets at individual men. Becket has Brother Thomas's vitals displayed on his Visuals, seeing the Knight is down with several wounds. "Thomas, hang in there. Help is on the way."

"Praise God!" Magallanes says. "Off the ship's bow, in the sky."

Becket hazards a look while he's moving aft. Sees a familiar silhouette that sends relief cascading through him. "'Bout time."

The drone-piloted dropship appears across the empty blue sky. It launches two telson rockets—red, long and thin anti-aircraft munitions. Both strike the sea before the ship and send up plumes of the fluid. The hardened chunks slap down all along the forward portion of the ship, chewing into ancient lizard bone and added materials alike. The sound makes a thousand pelting dribbles like a landslide.

Above the proud lizard skull, in the azure of the midday, the dropship aims nose to nose with the boat and dives towards them.

"Keep raining down fire, baby," Becket says as he reaches Thomas. Doesn't even slow down, just grabs him and drags him behind the cover Thomas was running for. "Keep raining down."

Magallanes rounds the cover as well and they go back-to-back with Thomas groaning at their feet. A second volley of telson rockets hits, splashing the ship with more extremely viscous chunks. Becket glances around the cover, sees the dropship closing in.

"None too soon," Magallanes says as he inventories his ammo. "I'm about dry."

"Me too," Becket says. "One full magazine left plus what I've got in the gun. You?"

"Less than that."

"Thomas here can donate," Becket says as he rifles through the groaning Knight's armament. He pockets a single magazine, hands one to Magallanes. Looks over the cover to the dropship. Says, "That thing is gonna come right over the top strafing. Get ready to jump, we've only got a split second— oh no. . ."

"What?"

The lizard skull opens its mouth with the kind of speed that looks like it's still alive. Boiling forth from it comes a gout of flaming material that sprays the entire distance and all over the dropship. Just waiting for it to swoop within range.

The burning vessel careens straight over the centerline of the Hhrothgar ship, bits of burning slag falling from it all the way. It wobbles on its horizontal axis. Kicks its nose steeply up into the air and twirls, almost out of control. Whatever the burning material is, its sticky and intensely hot. The dropship trails a thick blame plume behind it. Suddenly, it steeply descends towards the sea, careening with long tendrils of fire leaping off in its wake. It crashes into the sea and the fluid pops and chars as the incinerating dropship dies as poorly as their hopes of escape.

"I've never seen an op go this bad, this quickly," Magallanes says. "Lord, ease up on us, please."

"That is. . . unfortunate," Becket says as the silence around them leaves room for the burning, dying gasps of the dropship's remains. As they draw further away from it, the flames extinguish as every centimeter of it sinks lower and lower, consumed into the vast nothing. "Lord, be with us."

The clatter of weapons brings the Knights back. All around them, barrels at the ready. The leader walks up, in one hand the skull, in the other, a large weapon.

Becket nods to it, says through his translator, "That sure looks like it'll fire a rocket."

"Your friend seemed to think so as well," the leader says, his words tinged with triumphant pride. "For just a moment, anyway."

Becket eyeballs the skull in the leader's hand. A circle of crewmen trot around them. Surrounded. "You said it preaches to you?"

"It does," the leader says, and his men grab the Knights, greedily take their guns. "Come. Come and listen."

The Decapitated, the Betrayed, the Ugly

"Why do you worship this... this *thing*? Because of its magic?" Captain Melligrance asks as he ponderously examines the skull. The ship lists gently as it sails forever forward across the Devil's Throat Sea, the two remaining crates winched in fully now. The slave crate's ruins tugged up against the stern, like some mangled step up onto the deck from the thirsty maw of the desert brown sea around them.

The crew around them, maybe fifteen left, appear as nearly feral animals. The Knights can see in their eyes how they'd like to just kill them and have it be over with, but this captain is keeping them in check.

The captain stands there, appearing unaffected by the extreme loss he's suffered by the Knights before him. Stoic, yet rippling under the surface of his skin is a bloodlust. Brother Magallanes can see it, would send a message to his brothers about it in their Visuals had they not been stripped of their armor. Their universal translators are embedded devices that connect wirelessly to their helmets, so Magallanes can understand the captain's crude remarks.

A crewman came and set up a tripod with speakers on it. As they converse, the tripod blares their responses to each other in their native tongues. A translator of their own. The crewman kicked away the loose pile of armor strewn along the deck to make room for it. Magallanes looks about, sees the battle-damaged plates lying like shed carapaces.

It does makes it easier to see the wounds on Brother Thomas, though. Several penetrating gunshots along his lower half. Thank the Lord they have missed his spine. But everywhere else Thomas is blooming with red. He sweats against the pain of it all and cannot stand next to the others. He lays there on the deck, brutalized in the heat of the sun.

"It's not magic," Brother Becket answers, chin held high. "It's blessed. There's a difference."

"I know of your kind. This Order, you call it?" Melligrance says, and even those few words show he's heard enough to think it complete idiocy.

"The Knights of Those Washed in the Water and Blood from His Side."

"Thieves. A brotherhood of sniveling thieves. Sneaky, and stupid."

"It's not hypocritical at all of you to say that, being the guy who raided an unarmed monastery and pillaged it," Becket says. "Not to mention that group of Thovic you captured. Or did you—"

The captain slaps Becket like he's trying to knock teeth out. "On my ship, no one speaks to me that way."

"Let's you and me get off this ship, then," Becket says, and spits blood down along the captain's boot. Then stares at him defiantly.

Captain Melligrance smirks, and Becket can tell he's making sure his crew can see it. Obviously this Hhrothgar culture has a severe pecking order, and the captain is at the top of it for good reason. If he's disrespected by men he's taken captive, there will be punishments coming.

"Answer me," The captain says. "Why do you worship this?"

"We don't worship it. But it is sacred. And when evil men come along and murder for it, steal it, we want it back."

"Just as I want my slaves back," the captain says, leaning into Becket. Up close the leader smells like blood, though as far as Becket can discern, he is not injured. "Just as I want my slain crewmen back."

"Probably shouldn't have put them in a position to come between us and our relics then."

The captain smirks again. Becket doesn't think he's used to being sassed and isn't comprehending how to deal with it very well. He turns and paces, staring at the skull for a moment. Becket spits more blood off to the side. The crewmen are quiet; so are the other two Knights.

Finally, the captain raises his head, stops pacing. "It speaks to me as the wind rustles through it. I cannot understand it, but I am not imagining it. Why is it sacred? Because of this, the way it speaks?"

Becket rolls his head on his neck, says, "Rarely, our God—our Creator, and yours too, whether you acknowledge Him or not—will permit what our culture calls a Cephalophore. Our kind has been murdered for our faith. Some are beheaded, and the Cephalophores are those martyred who, after being decapitated, pick up their heads and continue preaching."

"A headless corpse acts as though it is not dead? And talks through a severed head?" The captain asks through dripping sarcasm.

"That's what you hold in your hands."

"Not even lunacy accounts for such terrific stupidity," the captain shouts to the cheers of his crewmen. "Your race and the races which follow your beliefs must be infected with an absolute dumbness the likes of which I cannot comprehend."

"Then why do you say it speaks to you with the winds?"

The captain pauses at that, stares. "It— no. . . no. I know it was the head of some preacher. And the wind rolling around inside, as I said plainly, I do not understand the sounds it makes. Because they are just noise."

"That may very well be the voice of God asking you to come to Him."

"Nonsense." The captain begins pacing again, then stops. "I am intrigued by it, though. It has a certain. . . beauty. But you . . . I thought it was a magical item to you. Something—a bone discovered, and like a lost naïve tribe, your kind attached silly superstitious beliefs to it. Like maybe it was used in some ritual to bring rain or a good harvest. But to think you ascribe to it such a miraculous thing as you do. . . a murdered man who picks up his head and preaches. My intrigue is quickly becoming disgust."

"Saint Charles the Thovic," Becket says, nodding at the skull. "The first and only known Cephalophore on your world. Beheaded long ago by a mob of unbelievers at the behest of the local governor. Many of the mob converted on that day."

"Thovics are all fools, and this Charles was one of them."

"He was an itinerant preacher, taken in after being orphaned and educated by Dominican preachers of my faith. He spent nearly a decade roaming all over the continent of Urasolsus back there—" Becket tilts his head to where the Thovics lived over the vast stretch of sea, "—preaching and teaching, baptizing, establishing churches. In the footsteps of a man we called Saint Paul on a planet called Earth. Until he was finally asked to die for his God. And he did so."

"Dying is dying."

"Wrong," Becket says. "Our God took on flesh and blood and dwelt among us, teaching His righteousness. He too, was murdered by the government. Accused by a mob with lies, labeled a criminal, he was executed. Died. But dying is not dying when yours is the authority over life and death. Our God rose from the grave and took His throne in the eternal afterlife."

"As I said, a terrific stupidity. An absolute dumbness."

"The mob swarmed Charles and forced him to his knees as they pressured the town governor to pronounce execution. He did, because apparently it was obvious it was going to be just Charles, or him *and* Charles if he said no. A nearby butcher shop loaned a knife to some crazed mobster and they wasted no time cutting his head off. And the corpse of Saint Charles the Thovic rose to his feet, severed head in hands, and began preaching. He walked through the stilled mob, and traveled three miles until he laid down at the foot of a shrine to the Blessed Virgin Mary—"

"At the Saint Albinetine's monastery," The captain says, eyes lighting up. "Yes, I saw this shrine. And I crushed it. I forgot; you worship some woman too."

"No, but we render her the honor she deserves."

"On your knees in supplication before the skulls of fools, non-existent gods, females. As I said: a terrific stupidity." The captain walks over a little way and finds a toppled container on the deck. Pockmarked with bullet wounds, but stable enough. Drags it over to where they are. "An absolute dumbness." He sets the skull on it, facing the Knights.

He turns, squints in the sunlight. Looks around at all angles until his eyes alight on something in the distance. He points to it, a grand gesture, and says, "Agravain! What is that over there?"

Becket and Magallanes watch as a Hhrothgar in the back of the crowd straightens up, collects himself. His uniform has designs on it similar to the captain's, but lesser in grandiosity. More than the others. Rank? Higher than crew, less than captain. "Aye, skipper? What do you ask?"

"That, over there, off the port bow. Not even a dhar away. What is it, my dedicated first mate?" The crowd mumbles, and the captain silences them. He wants his answer from Agravain, not some deckhand.

Agravain turns. Looks baffled for just a moment. Where the captain is pointing, he does indeed see something.

An apparition, maybe. A giant alien woman clothed in blue and white, just like the statue he saw outside the monastery. Her arms outstretched; she smiles. About her like clouds, are clusters of flowers. She is translucent—something only for his eyes. He blinks and she is gone. All that is left is a thin rock formation, like a line of crude stone, emerging from the merciless sea. Taller than the ship, casting a shadow that, at the right time of day, must be like a sun dial.

"It. . . uh. . . my captain it is. . . forgive me, as you know, I've just been from battle and I am. . . still foggy. I think I was hit, though not badly. I. . . "

"Answer me, First Mate Agravain."

The Hhrothgar clasps his hands in front of his belt to stop the trembling. He stares, his lips move silently. Finally, he clears his throat and says, "That is Skurrum Point, the sister rock to Hurrum Point, skipper."

The crewmen collectively groan. Someone in the crowd says, "As stupid as these god-men, me thinks."

Someone else says, "Stupider."

Captain Melligrance's eye twitches as he stares at his first mate. He walks over and grabs Agravain, who pulls away. The captain swings savagely at Agravain's head, pummeling him twice with haymakers. Agravain stumbles, shields himself. The crewmen around them grab ahold of the first mate and stand tense against him, look to their captain.

"There," The captain points to the bullet-wounded container he pulled next to Becket and Magallanes. The crew drag Agravain over to it. Force him down over it on his knees. Pin him there.

"I don't need a mob," the captain says with mirth. "I have a well-disciplined crew." They laugh, while Agravain pleads for his life.

"Skipper! Skipper! I was confused! I've sailed this sea a thousand times but never this route! I know I told you these things when you hired me, I just—"

The sound of the captain withdrawing his sword from his belt silences him. He holds it on display for the Knights, and the sun glints off it majestically.

"Our place in our culture is established by little else besides the quality of blood on your possessions. Whether that be your projectiles, your *gruntas*—" he twirls his blade to indicate it, "—or your bare fists. This grunta I won off a gladiator whose statue still stands outside the arena where he fought and killed for years. He was a slave, then became a sensation. Then earned his freedom through combat. Then stayed on because he loved blood and the money they paid him to spill it. And yet, I came along and was the end of all it. I wasn't even looking to fight.

We were at the same tap, drinking the same swill. And he thought I looked at him crosswise. If I did, I did not intend it. But he wanted my blood and called on me for it. I could not back down. And at the end, as he begged me for his life with his head locked in my arms, I enjoyed how slowly each of his vertebrae popped in half. And his sword, older than my great-grandfather and a fixture in that arena for its entire life, has traveled with me from then to today."

"And?" Magallanes says. "You don't mean to kill this man just because he can't readily name some rock formation out in the middle of nowhere."

"It is his job. You are not a sailor; you won't understand the need to know the seas upon which you travel. The depths, where it is safe to go, where you must avoid, the fastest routes, where the best fishing is at what season, the landmarks. To not know this is to not know life. To not know this is to endanger everyone else on your ship."

"Forgive him," Magallanes says with a shrug, as if the conclusion to such failure is so absurd that it is beyond even laughing at. "We know you're almost at port. Just fire him. Get somebody else. He's certainly humiliated by all this. But to—"

"Would you stand in his place, godman?" The captain asks. "If I were to execute you instead?"

"Do I have your word you'd spare him?"

The captain brightens. The crewmen jeer. "This—" he kicks Agravain and the beaten first mate rocks along the container, being pushed down into by the hands of his fellow crewmen, "this wretched garbage here, you would give your life so that I would not teach good order and discipline on my ship?"

"Mags—" Becket says.

"Would you give your word he would not be hurt if I did?" Magallanes asks. Stares straight into the eyes of the captain. Agravain bleats a whimper, blood from his face drawing tacky lines down the side of the container. He struggles meekly against the hands on him and is kicked again. Already a spot over his eye is swelling like a goose egg.

The captain can read the answer on the Knight's face. It is plain.

Magallanes says, "I am a Knight of the order of Those Washed in the Water and Blood from His Side. The Knights 15 13. *Greater love hath no man than this, that a man lay down his life for his friends.* If you have any honor, you'll spare him and take me."

"You question my honor?"

"I do."

Captain Melligrance grabs a handful of Agravain's quills and cuts them off with the grunta. Throws them Magallanes's feet. Then more. The Knights watch as Agravain struggles to remain stoic against the humiliation. Five more times and Agravain is bald, as was Marhault before him. "Stand, you embarrassing fool."

They let go of Agravain, and the captain shoves him over to where the Knights are. Agravain still bleeds freely from his head, and he cannot keep steady as he steps near them. He looks at Magallanes, though, then to the skull. Then back to the Knight. Squints in half-battered disbelief. "Lay down your life for your friends?"

Magallanes smiles and nods. "Yes. Christ taught that."

"I am not your friend."

"We're brothers. Brothers in Christ, and brothers are friends even when they don't get along."

Captain Melligrance sheaths his sword and waves a hand at Magallanes, says, "Feed him to the drive."

The crowd raves and grabs Magallanes, kicks him in the backs of his knees to make them buckle. Becket is held by the rest of the crew. He looks at his brother, then at the captain. The traitorous fury in the captain's eyes burns worse than any sun, and it stokes the same flames in Becket.

The crewmen begin to drag Magallanes away, and even the ruined Agravain shouts in protest. "His was to be a clean death, not the gears!"

"Honor is second to blood, you know that." The captain says. "Let him learn the price of questioning it."

Over the noise of the crowd, Becket makes sure he is heard. "Then I call on you for your blood, captain. Or back down and release all of us, including this shamed crewman. Answer me."

The crowd goes silent. The captain stands bolt still, his breathing deep and concentrated. "You challenge me?"

"I've seen your hypocrisy, your dishonor. Now all that's left is your cowardice," Becket says, making sure his tone insults the masculine character of the captain in front of all his subordinates. "Now, show that to me. You've shown those other characteristics easily enough."

Captain Melligrance snarls and roars. A bellowing and fierce sound, more at home with the bloodstained mouths of lions than with sentient beings who can build great ships. Throughout the entire battle, the Knights have not heard any of them make that sound.

Becket begins praying, though he is at peace. He looks to the other Knights, and now, this half-dead Hhrothgar first mate standing in their orbit. He locks eyes with Magallanes, says, "It's desperate, might as well make it ugly too."

The Rods, the Fists, The Grunta

Captain Melligrance stands on his side of a hastily drawn square along the deck made from slashes of chalk. Brother Becket on the other. In the center of the square are two metal rods, one thin like a lash and the other thick like a piece of construction stock. Smooth. Featureless. Just bare implements with which to use on one another.

Both combatants are shirtless, shoeless. Becket was made to tear his armor's under suit off at the knees, turning them into shorts and making them the same length as the captain's simple tunic wrap. Some kind of ceremonial Hhrothgar garb. Becket's foot sweeps aside another spent shell casing; he's noticed his side of the chalk square is towards the stern, where the shoot-out took place. Still littered with debris, spent casings, splinters and chunks torn out of the deck. The captain's side is near pristine in comparison. The captain cannot keep still, moving from one foot to the other and locking eyes on Becket. Rolling his shoulders, turning his head on his neck. Flexing his fists and curling them.

"Pre-fight indicators, no matter the species," Becket says to himself while he studies the warrior across from him. "Let's see. . . will the thin rod cut through your hide? Or do I need the heft of the thick one to just bash you? Which one is he gonna take? Both? Neither one has a good grip on it. Gonna be slick. Can I get both?"

Becket looks to the side, where Brothers Thomas and Magallenes are, down on their knees, hands behind their backs. Thomas looks to be in great pain, his wounds still bleeding. The submissive posture they have him in no doubt stressing the wounds, holding them open. The humiliated crewman—Agrabon? Abgravain? Whatever—beside them, same posture. Thrown away, cast into the ranks of the enemy.

Becket makes eye contact with Magallenes. Both nod. Thomas has his eyes closed, lips moving ever so slightly in prayer. Offering up his suffering to the Lord, the only thing he has to sacrifice at the moment. "May God use it to His glory," Becket says.

The humiliated crewman is staring directly at Becket. They make eye contact as well. Becket doesn't understand the Hhrothgar culture, their tics and subtilities. This man is blank faced, but his eyes communicate something. Fury at having been reduced to the same level as a Knight in the eyes of his species, maybe. Maybe he is imploring Becket to win and therefore grant him some of his good name back. Maybe he is trying to warn Becket of what is to come.

Becket looks at one of the guards standing beside them. The guard makes eye contact as well, smirks. Rotates one of his arms, and inside his fist is a long, thin shard of deck wood. When he sees that Becket is looking at his fist, he snaps the wood. The crack is distracting, and Becket has half a thought about why he would do that when he hears sudden movement.

The captain is thrusting forward. Becket reacts, lunges towards the rods.

†

The captain dives, rolls, and snatches up the thin rod as he passes by. Stops on his back and kicks, curls his body to his feet. Brother Becket has to dive as well, roll to the side and scramble at the thick rod. His fingers dig at it and the captain swings the lashing rod.

Becket grabs the thick rod but takes the lash across his hand. He doesn't let go, shoves himself backward as the captain tries to stomp on him. Becket harshly sucks air through his teeth. Gets to his feet. They square off. The captain barking, working his men up into a roaring froth. Becket watching the captain's shoulders, hips. Twitching, movement. Where the lashing rod is. The captain fakes a move, Becket reads it and doesn't react. The captain smiles viciously, playing.

"Saint Michael, pray for me," Becket says. "The Forty Martyrs of Sebaste, pray for me." The captain swings the rod in an upper cut.

Becket dodges, feels it slice through the air just next to his bare skin. "Saint Justo Takayama, pray for me."

Becket fakes going to his left and when the captain buys it Becket comes in from the right. Swings high, near the neck and head. The captain defensively tries to catch the rod but Becket yanks it back. The captain steps in deep, thrusts like a sword. Becket takes it off his belly and rotates hard to deflect. It scrapes his flesh. He swings again with the thick rod, hits the captain square along the side of his neck.

The captain falters, stumbles back a step. Recovers. Someone in the crowd behind Becket throws a small metal box no bigger than a hand at him. It hits his head, clatters with an empty sound onto the deck. Someone snatches it up, disappears into a handful of crewmen.

Captain Melligrance is pleased and comes at Becket like it's his grand move. Becket slaps at the back of his hand holding the rod. Knocks it back towards the captain. Swings his own rod down at the inside of the captain's elbow, immediately swings up towards his jaw. It scrapes the captain's skin and he backs off, comes back in. Tries the same grand slam and Becket redirects his palm with another strike. Swings at the captain again but he's learned. He pulls back, heaves around with the rod. Becket feels a sharp point behind his ear. A trickle of blood through his hair. He dodges to the side and parries the captain's attack, grabs his rod with both hands and tries to use it as staff the best he can.

The captain ducks in tight to Becket and thrusts his lashing rod through both of Becket's arms, grabs his own rod at the top and bottom and yanks back. Becket can feel the move trying to disarm him. He yanks back as well. They lock, their chests inches from one another. The captain growls, lifting a lip in a sneer.

"Got your boys cheating for you?" Becket taunts. "Afraid you can't win this without them?"

"You are weak."

So close, Becket head butts him. To both their credits, neither lets go of their rods. The captain shakes off the strike, though Becket can see he's fighting to act like it didn't land hard.

Becket says, "Me? Nah. I still hold the record for hand-to-hand combat at our training seminary."

"I am yet to be impressed." The captain yanks back hard. The rods clack and Becket can feel it run up the bones in his arms. Becket jerks his higher hand up the rod, sliding it in his palm. Stabs his thumb under the captain's little finger, tries to bend it backwards. The Hhrothgar finger joints roll with the bend and don't seem to have the same limitations human joints have. The captain shoves again, strikes Becket across the chest. They remain locked. Becket holds fast. Pulls the captain back in.

"I'm not worried about impressing you. I'm here to beat you."

"Oh?" The captain lets go with one hand, pulls his lashing rod out in a half swing down, thrusts back up trying to dig under Becket's ribs. Becket steps back, juts his rod out to deflect the strike. The lashing rod bounces off the thicker one and continues up to the captain's face. Nearly catches his eye. Becket hastens off to the side and swings hard.

The captain catches it in one hand, steps back and heaves Becket towards him. Becket is off-center by the attack anyway and can't fight the pull towards the captain without letting go. The captain throws a knee strike and Becket takes it full in the gut. Almost loses his grip on the rod.

The captain swings Becket by the rod, keeps him off balance. Becket has one hand on it, gritting his teeth in effort to not lose his grip. The captain moves to bite Becket's hand. Becket twists the rod just enough to where the captain's maw lands on metal. Becket throws a haymaker with his other arm and connects with the side of the captain's face. The warriors break apart, stumble back.

The captain shakes his head like a dog drying off and then leaps at Becket. Arms out, tackling. Becket kicks his legs backwards as he throws his upper body forward, effectively landing on top of the lunging captain. Drives him down. The captain's head hits the deck face first. Becket grabs the opposite side of the captain's body and throws two knee strikes into his ribs before the captain flails enough to shake Becket.

The Hhrothgar swings a sweeping stroke with the lashing rod, catches Becket across the belly. A bright red line rises to the surface. Both men down on their knees, the captain tackles Becket and lands on top of him. The heavy rod falls off to the side and rolls. Becket works an arm under the captain's arm, locks the elbow. The captain tries to bite Becket's throat so he shoves his chin at his chest protectively. Becket feels one leg free and wraps it around the leg the captain is using to push against the deck and keep him pinned into Becket.

With Becket's free arm, he starts punching the captain in the eye. Repeatedly, a deliberate attempt to get the captain's defensive instincts to take over. The captain takes the lashing rod like a dagger and stabs down. Becket scrunches off to the side just enough to let the rod jam into the deck instead. The captain pulls on it to free it, but the rod bends. Becket feels his other leg free enough to where he throws another knee strike between the captain's legs.

The captain doesn't react the way a human man would, and Becket groans. He strikes again, no better. The captain struggles against the rod but bends it more. Becket arches his back, then flops down. Arches again and the captain responds by moving his body, taking Becket's bait. As the captain moves, Becket frees both arms and kicks to roll over. Wraps his arms around the captain's neck in a choke hold.

The Knight squeezes tightly. The captain laughs; wherever his breaths are coming from, they're not affected by the hold. The captain is face down with Becket on his back. Becket tries a knee strike from the side. Not good enough. He plants his feet wide, gets a good wide base. Uses his whole upper body to try and roll the captain. Pin him.

The captain spits at Becket's face and manages to stand up, grabs Becket by both his elbows and flips Becket over his head.

Becket loses the choke hold but lands on his feet. Spins awkwardly, fist trailing behind him in a haymaker. The captain catches it and wrenches him around. Becket moves with the motion, stepping into it. He grabs the captain by his upper arm and flows through the movement, taking the captain off his feet. Tosses him a few meters away.

Becket rushes to his dropped rod only to see a crewman grab it. He turns to the bent lashing rod stabbed in the deck. He takes hold of it as the captain regains his feet. Becket heaves once against the bent angle of the rod and it snaps in half. Becket turns with his broken piece as the captain comes forward, fists in the air.

"Those are some big mitts you got there," Becket says as he raises his own fists in a boxer's stance. Rod in one hand.

"They will have your blood on them," The captain says as he steps in closer. He tests Becket with a light jab, Becket noting which is the captain's offhand so he can beware of his strong hand. Becket ducks to one side and the other, feeling out his style. Becket throws a solid straight jab, the captain's guard blocking it. The captain throws a good swing and Becket dips away. Comes back in and kicks at the captain's ankle. Gets a good one. The captain can't help but take his weight off that foot. Snarls with the pain.

From the crowd someone throws another harassing piece of detritus at Becket's head. Becket sees it out of the corner of his eye and dodges. The captain swings again with a haymaker and connects solidly with Becket's head.

The Knight sees stars and loses his footing. Falls. Drops the piece of lashing bar. Tries to recover but the captain is on him, getting him in his own choke hold. Becket sucks in a deep breath even as the arms wrap around him. The captain opens wide his jaws and latches them on

Becket's head. His scalp comes alive with the teeth biting down. The crowd of crewmen go wild, the bloodlust in the air severe.

Becket down on his knees, plants his legs widely. Already blackness edging in on his vision. His lungs burn. His whole body taxed; he has but a few moments left in his reserves. He can hear how tired the captain is also.

Becket has one hand trying to shove up between the captain's strangling arm, the other throwing elbow strikes behind him. The captain's long quills jangle against Becket's elbow, and he contorts his arm around. Grabs a handful. Yanks hard. Remembering how the humiliated crewman reacted to having his quills cut off, Becket risks the maneuver hoping it will cause pain. A reaction to the attempted humiliation.

And it does.

The captain pulls his jaws off Becket's head, going with the jerk. Becket tugs with everything he has left, feels some quills come loose between his gripping fingers. The captain yowls in agony and throws Becket to the deck. Races up and kicks him in the back along his ribs like he's trying to set a record. Becket rolls with the kick, comes to a stop on his side facing the raging captain. The captain runs forward again, readying a second kick. As he does Becket catches his foot and rolls with it, twisting the leg. Hammers the ankle.

Something fleshy snaps in the captain's leg and he collapses. As their roll finishes Becket uses the momentum to add to a haymaker he barrels down with on the captain. His knuckles make a battering ram across the Hhrothgar jaw. Becket feels his finger bones scream to the point of breaking; punching that jawline is like punching a steel bar.

Becket stumbles back, trips over the remaining piece of lashing bar still stabbed in the deck. He grabs it with both hands and heaves, bending. The thing releases and he comes up with it, disappointed with how short the length is. He straightens his body and sees the captain trying to shake off the punch, trying to get back to his feet with whatever tendon or ligament snapped in the roll.

Becket lunges forward, driving the lashing rod down. The captain swings an arm up to deflect it but takes the point on his palm. The rod drives through, appears on the other side. The captain reacts to the wound and swings his other arm. Hits Becket but his training still responds. He rolls with it, deflecting what he can. Shooting up to his feet, one hand still on the rod, Becket grabs the exposed end, wet with blood. Twists it forcefully inside his hand. The captain stomps once at Becket's feet and misses. Another piece of broken trash flies out of the crowd, hits Becket in the face. He loses his wet grip. The captain stomps again and grinds his heel into the top of Becket's foot. The Knight grunts and nearly loses his balance. Lets go of the bloody end. The captain kicks him away, yanks the rod from his palm and throws it high and away in agonizing repulsion. It twirls in a high arc and goes overboard.

Th captain kicks at Becket again and catches him in the back of a knee. Becket buckles and the captain moves over to the crowd. Becket stumbles away, falls against the overturned box over which Captain Melligrance de-quilled Agravain. As he bumps into it, the Cephalophore skull rolls and falls into his lap.

The captain limps hard to the edge of the crowd. From somewhere within it he withdraws his grunta. He twirls the blade; the sunlight glints off it. He cannot hide his burning limp as he stalks towards Becket.

"Stay there, let's finish this." The captain commands. Becket smiles at the audacity of it. He starts to get up and the thick rod hurls at him from the crowd. It hits across his face, and he crumples. The rod bounces away and clatters to the deck, rolls off into the crewmen's line. Magallanes, Thomas and even the humiliated Agravain shout about the dishonorable conduct. The nearby crew beat and kick them, commanding them to be silent. They are not.

Captain Melligrance closes the gap, and a disoriented Becket cannot get up. "Lord, use my death to purchase the lives of my friends, even this Hhrothgar they've cast down with us. Please let me spend eternity with You in glory. I love you."

As he prays, blood runs from Becket's mouth. The captain looms over him, mocking. "Yours is the only god I have ever heard of that thinks failure is success. What a joke upon you, that you worship such a thing."

Not steady on his feet himself, the captain takes in a deep breath and heaves the grunta upwards. The wind blows with a sudden strength across them, so much so that the captain rocks some in his footing and the weight of the grunta shifts in his grip, then topples. He corrects his stance, but the weapon's weight causes him to lower his taxed arms. He rests the tip of the grunta on the deck as he builds back up some strength.

The gust rolls through the skull, and Becket can hear a voice. Becket listens as his God speaks to him. He smiles and relaxes. The captain turns his head tries to listen, words he cannot understand coming to him from some long-dead piece of bone.

In an astonished voice, the captain asks, "What does it say?"

Becket sits up straighter, sighs. "It is God. He wants you to convert. He wants you with Him for all eternity. We are brothers. Act like it."

Captain Melligrance's face curls in disgust. "I am not so weak as to believe you."

"It is the truth."

"Please, fool. Even to the death, you play that card. *Join your God. Be brothers.* Stay your execution is what you mean. You lost, and at the hands of your death you use this relic to try and scam me."

"No, He wants to be in your friendship. All of you. He can demand your lives today—right now—if He should wish it, but He instead asks you to come to Him of your own volition. Why not? Why not live correctly?"

"Silence!" The captain thrusts his grunta at Becket's heart. The Cephalaphore skull catches the blade in its eye socket, and Becket, with the bones in his grasp, twists violently. The grunta rotates in the captain's hand, unbelieving that mere bone would stop his weapon. Becket sweeps the captain's bad leg and he topples over. Becket swings his open fist in a wide arc down at the captain. The edge of his hand chopping along the captain's face just below his eyes. A crunching sound comes up out of his face and Becket scrambles to his feet.

Becket grabs the grunta with his free hand, savagely chops down at the captain. It strikes hard into the table by his head, cleaving a wedge into it. The blade stops just short of Captain Melligrance's throat; the Hhrothgar neck quivering with a held breath and the rush of adrenaline burning down in his veins. The blade sings with a high-pitched twang, vibrating with the sudden stop of violence as it is wedged into the table.

Both men stay still for a moment, letting the killing stroke evaporate into the wind like so much smoke. Becket clears his throat and says, "Yield."

The captain stares at him for a moment, then looks down to the blade so close to his flesh that errant sweat beads running down his neck are already beginning to collect on the metal.

"Yield and we'll be on our way. Easy. God still speaks to you, wants you with Him."

The captain smiles weakly. "I have your word?"

"You do."

"Then we agree."

Becket nods. "So be it." He steps back, pulling the grunta with him. He nods at the captain and is struck from behind so hard he falls forward. The captain stands, considers the Cephalophore skull now in his hand, picks up his grunta and barks.

"You wanted examples of my dishonor, my cowardice, my lies. Here they are," he says, and he walks over to the other Knights as they push Magallanes forward.

Captain Melligrance swings the grunta and the Knight collapses. The Hhrothgar follows some object on the deck for just a moment before snickering and gently kicking at it.

Magallanes's head rolls over to Becket. The captain thumps down to a seat on the cleaved table, points at the head. "Think he'll rise up and start preaching?"

The Vile, The Fury, The Glory

Brother Becket looks away from his brother's head, feels the deep hurt inside. He tries to counter the immediate thoughts by telling himself that Brother Magaellenes died helping to save the Thovic, save his friends, stop evil, rescue priceless relics. All noble things. As his Savior has said, greater love hath no man than this, that a man lay down his life for his friends.

Victimized by a betrayer. Becket swallows hard.

Captain Melligrance leans in, spits on the head. Says, "Are you berating yourself? You should be. He died because of you."

Becket looks up, matches eyes with the captain. Beaten, limping, successful only by the aid of his lackies. Becket spits on him. "He died because your treachery knows no bounds."

"You all will," the captain says as he stands.

"I'm pretty sure that grunta belongs to me now, cap," Becket says as the crew forces him down to his knees beside a suffering Thomas and Agravain. "But thank you for showing your cowardice just like I thought you would."

"He who dies by it does not get to claim it," the captain says, coming to a halt within swinging distance of the two remaining Knights and Agravain. Thomas is more fully awake now, no doubt the brilliance of the pain has sharpened his senses, kept him from his stupor.

"Your dishonor forfeits it," Becket says. "I beat you, and your boys jumped in to save you. You lost."

"Much like your silly god, you define winning in a very strange way," the captain looks around, pointedly making sure Becket can see him staring at the Knights as they are being forced into a supplicating position to be killed. "Am I wrong?"

"I'm starting to think you never won that grunta at all."

"Oh?"

"The way you fight, you probably stole it while the rightful owner was in the bathroom."

"I'm not even looking forward to killing you," the captain says. "I just want you to shut up."

"Do it, then, coward, while your crew holds us down."

"Finally, you say something I think is intelligent," the captain says. He lifts the sword and peers over Becket's shoulder. His eyes go wide, and he throws himself to the ground as gunfire erupts from behind them. Several in the crew fall motionless, snapping this way and that with the impacts.

Becket dives, grabs Thomas and Agravain. Looking behind him, sees the surfaced hatch from the submersible and a Thovic unleashing fury with a fully automatic weapon from the vessel's weapons closet. The crew on the deck scrambles like a beehive in smoke; confused, poisoned.

Becket shoves Thomas and Agravain towards the submersible. "Go, I'll get the relics cut free!" Agravain pulls away, darts to the overturned table. He squats and comes back up with the Cephalophore skull.

He stumble-runs over to Becket amidst the gunfire—now being returned from the few remaining crew. Looks the Knight in the eye, says in a voice like he cannot believe his own words, "I. . . I heard it too. . . His voice. This God of yours. He is mine as well?"

Becket smiles, slaps him on the shoulder. Can recognize in his eyes the truth of his claim. "He is. Go."

Agravain gathers up Magallanes's corpse and drags it to the submersible. Two of the Thovic come on board the ship and provide covering fire as the repentant Hhrothgar, utterly ruined for his own culture now, boards.

Thomas appears with the rocket launcher the captain was using as well as a harmonica-style clip that has four mini-rockets still in it. The harmonica clip loads on the left side of the launcher, feeds in far enough to position the next rocket with each trigger pull.

He slaps it in place, aims at the first gearbox and wench holding the relics crate and fires. The box disintegrates in a hail of shrapnel. The tow chain goes slack and then begins to droop down into the sea.

"Get the next one!" Becket shouts as he runs over to the chain. He grabs it, feels the explosion's heat on the broken link. Drags it across the deck towards the submersible as Thomas fires at the second crate. It explodes as well.

"Thomas—" Becket begins as the captain reappears from around the deck and strikes at him with the grunta. Becket rolls, dropping the chain. He sweeps at the captain's bad leg but misses. The captain switches the sword in his hands to plunge it into Becket's heart. Drops his body weight down and thrusts. Becket catches the captain's forearms and pushes up, holding the blade just off his chest.

"The cost of everything that has happened today rests on you, god-man," the captain growls under his breath as he heaves downward. "You owe me in blood. . . you owe me so much in blood."

"I've offered you peace. I've offered your life to you. Even my God spoke to you. You reject everything of true value," Becket says, pushing up. He knows he is going to lose, can feel his muscles burning with exertion and still the grunta blade descends a fraction a second.

Becket, on his back, tilts his head and sees Thomas dragging the other chain to the submersible. Handing it off to a Thovic. Turning to see him, then put his head down and starts running, rocket launcher still in hand.

Gunfire strafes across him one more time, and Thomas blooms with fresh wounds. Falls. The captain laughs with a cruelty Becket has not heard since his imagination pictured the Garden of Eden and Eve eating from the forbidden fruit. In Becket's mind, the serpent laughed the same way.

"Down to one, I see," the captain taunts. Pushes harder. The Thovic and Hhrothgar crew finish it out, only sporadic gunfire form either.

But there's no clear line of sight from the submersible to Becket. No covering fire. No saving. It is only he, the captain, and the blade.

Becket closes his eyes and breathes in as deeply as he can. Prays to his guardian angel for intercession. Feels the calmness of angelic hands laying upon him. Feels a warm droplet of divinity on his soul. Feels the blade tip touch his chest, pierce it. Becket lets it enter; the captain has angled it to run between his ribs. Once Becket is sure it's between the bones, he opens his eyes, winks. Says, "You know, it worked with the eye socket. . ."

"What?"

Becket summons everything he has, curls his legs up onto the deck and twists his body. His ribs catch the grunta and turn it in the captain's hands, stealing from his grip. Becket shoves up off the deck, one hand swinging down to grab the knee of the captain's bad leg. Grips and pulls. The captain howls and loses his bearing.

Becket pushes to his feet and pulls the grunta from his chest. The captain stares in open disbelief. Becket slashes the captain across his belly with it. Opens him wide. The captain falls over, miserably protecting his waist. On his feet, Becket says, "I'm a clone. Straight out of a lab. One of the things they did to me at a fetal level was tweak the density of my bones. This sword will shatter before one of them breaks. Thanks, by the way," Becket says as he twirls the grunta around in his grip. "I'll take good care of it."

He reaches over and grabs the chain. Sprints across the deck to the submersible, tosses it to the Thovic. Runs back a few meters to the pile of Magallanes's armor and digs through it. Comes up with the CQ4 detonator. Moves to Thomas, picks him up, drags him to the submersible and hands him off as well.

Captain Melligrance tries and fails to rise to his feet. His gut wound severe, he cradles an arm over it and spends all his energy breathing steady, controlling his body's descent into blinding panic. He stares at Becket and seethes hatred.

Becket pauses on the aft deck. Makes eye contact with the captain and he holds up the detonator. Points it at the nuclear drive paddling the ship. A communication passes between them; fierce warriors finally determining their inevitable outcome.

The drive explodes, shatters every plank of wood in the vessel. Both driven lizard legs uncouple from the gearboxes and topple into the sea. The ship breaks fore to aft along the keel, then along the transom in several places. Like an earthquake devastating a fault line, the ship snaps into pieces.

Becket and the Thovic gunners get back on board their craft. The submersible backs away, Becket, beaten, bloody, half-dead, stands vigil on the open hatch as the Hhrothgar plundering vessel slows to a stop. Crumbled, jagged, it sinks in pieces.

Captain Melligrance uses everything to rise to his feet, so weak but still delusionally proud. One hand across his unzipped gut, he stands there as the Devil's Throat Sea creeps in around him, a flood of swallowing fluid. Becket, maybe ten meters away, floats on his safe patch of submersible. The captain, scoundrel and betrayer, bloodlusting and defeated, stares defiantly at the Knight. The sea reaches his thighs, and he does not move.

Becket finds his eyes and remains there. The captain up to his nearly disemboweled waist in the sea. Becket feels the weight of the grunta in his hand, sees the two crates of relics, art and miscellaneous items begin to shift under the pull of the submersible. Coming towards him. There is virtually no Hhrothgar ship left. No crew to speak of. Maybe some of them are clamoring onto pieces of the ship, trying to fight the physics of the dilatant fluid. Maybe some have found a lifeboat. Most found hot gunfire.

Captain Melligrance is up to his chin the Devil's Throat Sea, tilts his head back to keep his death-gaze at the Knight a moment longer, and Becket locks eyes with him as the vile captain dips below the surface. His quills float for a moment more before they too vanish.

Becket looks up in the sky, waiting for the *Saint Laurence* to finish their repairs and come fetch him and the others. He looks down the short ladder at a passenger standing at the base of it. The humiliated crewman, Agravain.

"Brother?" He says, trying out the word. "Brother in Christ?"

"Yes, I am."

"The other warrior with you, the one shot and shot again?"

"Brother Thomas. Yes."

"He is in what we are calling medical on this tiny contraption. He is still not dead."

Becket laughs. "Still not dead. I'll take that as a good thing."

Agravain shrugs. "I hope he remains not dead, yes. There has been a heavy cost today."

"There has."

"I am . . . thankful, though."

"Oh yeah?"

"Before today, before I heard the skull, saw you and your fellow warriors. . . I had many holes in my. . . in here." He taps on his chest with a fist wrapped in a rosary. Becket hadn't noticed that before. "They feel better, so much more than they ever were when I was following. . . the captain. Our way of life. I guess, better than when I was following the lies."

"The lies. That's a good way to put it." Becket nods, takes another look around the flat sea. "We try to live the truth here, in Christ Jesus."

"This. . . whatever this is, I want it." Agravain says. He is cradling the Cephalophore skull. "My distant cousin Bav, he found it. And I wish to as well."

Becket points to it, says, "Saint Charles the Thovic, he's a good place to start. Let's go to medical and I can tell you why he loved Christ so much. . . why he died for Him, and now lives in Him." Becket meagerly climbs down inside and shuts the hatch.

Afterward

After we finished *Stigmata Invicta,* Joe suggested we write short stories and get them to readers between novels. On the last page of *SI,* Commander Brigid tells Brother Gonzaga they're getting a new Knight by the name of Brother Becket. They're getting him because his other team didn't survive a mission. That would be a cool story to write.

On YouTube, Ryan's children used to watch a science teacher turned public figure named Steve Spangler. Once, Spangler was on the Ellen DeGeneres Show and demonstrated a mixture of corn starch and water that remained a fluid until force was exerted against it, causing it to act as a solid. On the show, they filled a giant tank with the mixture and asked guests from the audience to run across it. The guests stomped barefoot across the surface of the corn starch mixture, and as long as they kept moving, they made it to the other side without falling in. That idea became the basis for the Devil's Throat Sea.

Cephalophores (from the Greek for "head-carrier") are a category of martyr. Depending on your source, you'll read everything from Cephalophores being depicted in iconography or statues as simply holding their decapitated heads, to the head continuing to speak for a moment after being severed, to the extreme of our saint here. Saint Charles the Thovic, whose body picked its head up and continued to preach and walk for a certain distance. We liked the miraculous nature of that. It Saint Charles the Thovic's display.

Captain Melligrance, Agravain and several others of the Hhrothgar crew got their names from Arthurian legend as Ryan read Roger Lancelyn Green's *King Arthur and His Knights of the Round Table.* He kept a list of names to use later. During rewrites, new Hhrothgar crew were added, but those guys didn't get the Arthurian treatment.

We wish to give huge thanks to Doug Fitzpatrick and G.T. Barvick, who have steadfastly read earlier drafts of the story and given feedback. Doug was nice. G.T. made Ryan cry.

As always, a tremendous thank you to Patrick Sayles for generating the cover art. Many thanks to Paula Hays at Floralies Creative for the layout and lettering. And a big thank you to Catherine Lueckenotte for the copy editing. She didn't edit this afterwards, so if there is a grammatical error here, it's on us, not her.

God bless you all, and please stick around. There's more coming, and rather quickly.

CMC

Carl Michael Curtis is the pen name of Catholic authors Joe Ralston and Ryan Sayles. *Stigmata Invicta* was their first work together, and the beginning of the *Knights 1513* series. *Vindicare Hope* serves as a prequel side story to *Stigmata Invicta*, alongside the upcoming prequel novel, *Rescued ex Inferna*.

Joe Ralston has spent his life collecting memories, stories, and experiences. From his days as a ranch cowboy, riding bulls, working as a bouncer, soldier, police officer, doing executive protection, and as a construction scuba diver to being an adventurer and explorer, he has dedicated himself to the pursuit of adventuring.

Ryan Sayles married his high school sweetheart. Through his wife's selfless generosity, his quiver has been filled with seven arrows. He drove boats for the military and policed in bad neighborhoods. Now he is a tradesman. He's published several secular novels in the crime genre.